W9-DFI-117

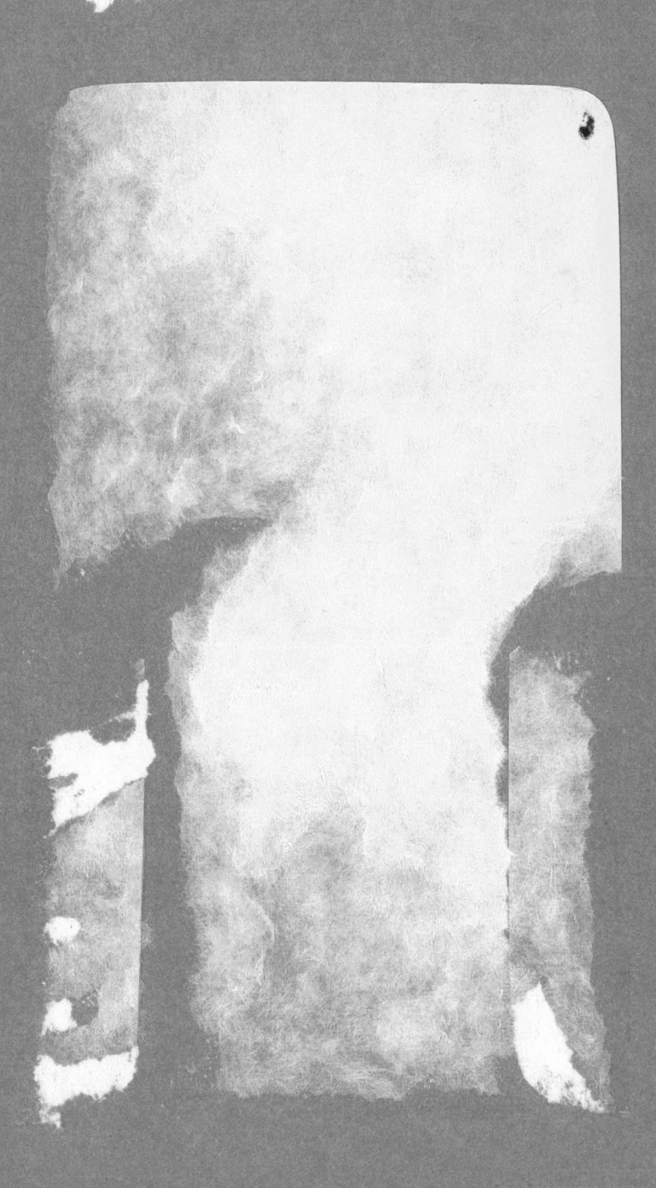

The House of the Four Winds

Selected and Translated by Miriam Morton

FIERCE AND GENTLE WARRIORS,
stories by Mikhail Sholokhov

SHADOWS AND LIGHT, stories by Anton Chekhov

THE FIRST SONG, by Semyon Rosenfeld

THE HOUSE OF THE FOUR WINDS,
by Colette Vivier

The House of the Four Winds

By Colette Vivier

Translated and Edited by Miriam Morton

Doubleday & Company, Inc.
Garden City, New York

Original French title:
La Maison des Quatre-Vents
Copyright *Editions G.P.*
Bibliothèque Rouge & Or
Paris

LIBRARY OF CONGRESS CATALOG CARD NUMBER 69–17861

PRINTED IN THE UNITED STATES OF AMERICA

To Lewis

M. M.

Foreword

My name is Denis. I knew Michel, the hero of this book, in 1943, and what we are now reading in our French history books, he lived through day after day. It was the most terrible period of the German occupation. The Nazis had been in France for three years, and no one could yet predict that one year later they would be driven out of our country.

There were shortages of everything: there was hardly anything to eat, little to wear, and no fuel during that winter. People stood in line for hours at the stores, with their ration tickets—the DX, BX, DZ—which entitled them to a small weekly ration of dried vegetables or a meager piece of beef. The vitamin wafers distributed in the class-rooms were the only treat the school children knew.

Lists of hostages who had been executed were posted on building walls. All those with Jewish names—men, women, and little children—were sent to concentration camps, from which many never returned.

Some of the French accepted all this and co-operated

with the Germans; they were called "collaborators." Others, of whom there were only a few, actually fought on the side of the enemy—they were called the *miliciens* (militiamen) by their countrymen. But most of the people refused to accept the occupation. Underground leaflets circulated everywhere; neighbors gathered in each other's homes to listen secretly to the news broadcasts from England. Action groups were soon formed all over France; they were the *Résistance,* the resistance. Some of the resisters were called *maquisards*—the ones who operated against the invaders in the countryside. Many of the resisters, like Daniel in this true story, paid with their lives for their heroism, and many, like Michel, have not forgotten their noble example. The ones who remember the dark years know that the word "peace" is the most beautiful of all words.

It was a time of war. . . .

Translator's Note

In France, the weekday off for school children is Thursday, not Saturday.

During the German occupation of France, the enemy were usually referred to in conversation as "they."

PRONUNCIATION GUIDE

er at the end of a word or name is pronounced like *ay* in stay; *ou* is pronounced like *oo* in pool; *ch* like *sh* in shoe; *i* like *ee* in seen. Very often the last letter of a word or name is not sounded.

Michel–Mishel
Sellier–Selleeay
Moscot–Mosco
Minet–Meenay
Gourres–Goor
Queline–Kuleen
Ménard–Maynar
Barroux–Barroo
Carpot–Carpo
Gilles–Geel

Contents

24 Street of the Four Winds 15

The Pirates of the Résistance 42

Christmas Eve 68

Daniel 93

Fanfan's Teddy Bear 115

George 135

The Liberation 155

The House of the Four Winds 182

Conclusion 188

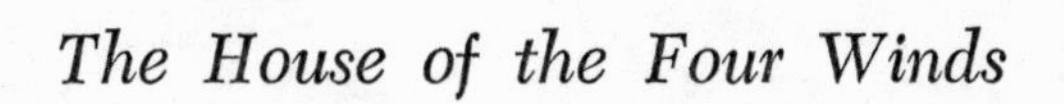

The House of the Four Winds

24 Street of the Four Winds

(Paris, 1943)

"What are you doing, Michel?" asked Madame Sellier, coming into the dining room from the kitchen, dishcloth in hand. "Don't tell me you're still playing! What about your problems?"

Michel quickly dropped the lid of the box containing his small printing set and answered guiltily, "I'm through with the first one, and the second . . . well, I just can't get the answer for that one. But it's not my fault!"

"Not your fault? All you have to do, son, is try a little harder. But you'll finish your homework later. I need you now—you have to go down to the store to get some milk for Fanfan."

"What about Norette?" Michel grumbled.

"Norette went down at five o'clock. The milk hadn't come yet. Now it's your turn. Here is the money; the blue pitcher is on the cupboard. And be sure to bundle up—it's very cold out."

Madame Sellier returned to the kitchen, walking with her usual light step. She was a slender, pleasant-looking woman with a worn face. Her husband had been a prisoner in Germany for the past three years. She was barely making ends meet by taking in sewing and doing alterations for a haberdasher in the Vaugirard neighborhood. She had gotten so used to concealing her sorrow from the children that they never imagined that she could be weary or discouraged. Besides, they didn't even think about it—their mother was always there, like a strong pillar, and she seemed to have no existence apart from them.

Michel put on his coat, still grumbling. As he was about to walk out the door he retraced his steps, intending to take his printing box with him. "I can't leave it here," he thought, "with that Norette around, sticking her nose into everything."

It looked like just an ordinary box. Its four corners were dented, and the picture on the lid, representing a small boy waving a magazine, was smeared with ink. Michel tied a heavy string around the box, made three neat knots and, hesitating a moment, slid it under the cupboard instead of taking it with him. This done, he ran down the stairs, pitcher in hand.

Outside it was a dark December night. All that could be discerned in the street was the light reflected by the crusted snow, which was marked with footprints. Michel took a few running slides over the frozen snow to stay warm, but he slipped and nearly lost his balance. Another wobble and he would have fallen and broken the pitcher. "What an idea to send a boy for milk when there is a girl in the family!" he said to himself. Besides, having to hold a pitcher in one hand made it pretty impossible for a boy to cup his hands and whistle through his fingers.

At last he reached the store. A black curtain covered its window from the inside, but a narrow streak of light, which filtered through the slightly open door, made dimly visible about twenty people standing in a close queue. Michel gritted his teeth with exasperation. What a crowd! It meant that he'd have to wait at least a quarter of an hour for his turn. He took his place at the end of the long line, looking very annoyed.

"Say, are the DX stamps for dehydrated vegetables?" asked a short woman standing in front of him. She asked the question of no one in particular. A voice coming from way up front answered her, "The DX?—those ration stamps are out of date, my dear woman, now it's the DY."

"Good gracious!" exclaimed the little woman. "Are you sure? I thought the DX were the right ones. How in the world do they expect us to keep track of all this?"

"What a life!" someone nearby took up the complaint. "At least if these dried vegetables were good! But they're as hard as rocks. The other day I soaked some beans—kept them in water for forty-eight hours—but it was a waste of time—they didn't get a bit softer. And the pork, why that's even worse! Last time the sausages smelled so bad that my husband refused to eat them. I had to give them to my cat. It's a rotten existence! And when will this misery end? Two months ago we were told, 'Wait till Christmas, 1943!' Well, here it is Christmas . . . the English . . . the Russians . . ."

A third voice joined the conversation, warily, "Still, there was an announcement over the radio this morning . . ."

"What radio?" asked a bulky man who had just joined

the queue; he was standing behind Michel. The hesitant voice didn't answer him. The pitchers and pots rattled. The people in line fell silent.

"This is no time to be saying things in public," the little woman whispered after a while. "The spies—they seem to be everywhere! For instance—just listen to this —last week . . ."

But Michel had stopped listening. He had noticed, standing near the door to the store, his classmate Mourette, a fat and greedy boy who often stole Michel's vitamin wafers in class when he wasn't looking. But now, since Mourette was the only other boy in the line . . .

Michel said to the short woman, "Please, madame, would you mind my place for me a minute, just for a tiny minute?"

"I don't see why not," she replied.

He made his way to the door. When Mourette saw him, his moonface beamed with pleasure. "Hi there," he called out. "Are you doing forced labor, too?"

"You said it! Isn't it freezing! By the way, did you do your problems for tomorrow? What answer did you get for the second one?"

"The one about the train? Let me think . . . something like 1327 kilometers an hour. No, wait, it was 1387 kilometers."

"That many?—1387 in an hour? That's impossible for a train!"

Mourette picked his nose, deep in thought, and then expressed his final opinion about the matter: "It may be impossible for a real train, but that one isn't real—it's only a train in an arithmetic problem."

"That makes no difference, stupid! You didn't do it right!"

"Is that so! What about you?—what answer did *you* get?"

"Me? . . . Me? . . . Oh, bother! I don't care! I'm not going to do it—not that one!—Monsieur Touron can say whatever he wants to. Anyhow, he had no business giving us such a tough problem only three days before Christmas vacation!"

Two women came out of the store now. The queue moved forward. Mourette stepped inside and Michel was about to follow him in.

"Hey, you, over there!" a man farther down on the line yelled. "You don't belong up there, you sneak!"

Michel looked back at the man, and pleaded, "Oh, monsieur, my hands are freezing! And if you only knew all the hard arithmetic problems I have to do tonight, for school . . . Isn't that true, Mourette?"

"Sure," Mourette answered with great conviction.

"All right, let's move!" the man said, grinning knowingly. "Let's stop talking about it. Go on in but make it snappy, you foxy one."

"Thanks, monsieur!" Michel cried, his eyes beaming with the easy victory.

He bought his quart of milk and, after taking leave of Mourette at the corner, turned his steps toward his house, whistling.

"Well, you certainly took your time about it," his mother said when he came in. "I hope you weren't too cold. Come quickly, warm up at the stove while it's still hot, and make sure you've closed the door tightly so that the heat doesn't escape."

Norette was setting the table for dinner, and Fanfan, thumb in mouth, was watching the pot boil on the stove.

"We're having cabbage soup," the little one informed his big brother. "Mommie found a cabbage. It's yummy —cabbage soup!"

"Oh, that one! He thinks everything is yummy as long as it is something to put in his mouth," Norette said affectionately. Then, turning to Michel, she asked, "What are you doing at the stove? Don't you upset that soup!"

"Mother told me to warm my hands here. I can't very well do it without moving the pot out of the way!"

"But you'll spill the soup! . . . Oh! Boys! . . ."

"That's enough out of you, bossy—don't act as if you are junior mother around here. It's enough that *I* had to go for the milk! . . . What else is there besides cabbage soup?"

"The rest of the noodles."

"That tastes good!" said Fanfan.

"That tastes very bad," said Michel. "I've had all the butterless noodles I can stand!"

"You'll eat them just the same," predicted Norette. "And now put the soup back over the flame or it'll get cold. No, not that way, lower the gas and . . ."

Madame Sellier came into the kitchen and said, interrupting Norette, "Children, let's hurry with the dinner. The Moscots are coming over at eight to listen to the British broadcast with us, and it's already . . . goodness! . . . it's ten to eight! Maybe the clock is fast. Listen, I think there's someone at the door. Who could it be? Norette, please go and see."

Norette ran to open the door and came back followed by a pale little girl wearing a gray coat that she had outgrown, and under which her pink apron was showing.

"It's Solange," Norette said, glad to see her friend.

"So it is," said Madame Sellier. "Come in, Soso. What is it?"

"I came to ask you to lend me a little salt," Solange answered shyly. "I thought I still had some, but there isn't a grain left."

"Of course you may have some, but what are you going to do with it?"

"It's for my noodles."

"We're going to have noodles, too," Fanfan informed her, taking the thumb out of his mouth for the moment.

Madame Sellier opened the salt box. "The salt is coarse and gray, you know. . . . Tell me, Soso, have you heard anything from Alain?"

Solange lowered her head, trying not to show the tears that welled up in her eyes. She was an orphan, and her brother Alain, with whom she lived, had joined a *Résistance* group. The child hadn't seen him for two weeks, and every evening she hoped he would come home to her.

Madame Sellier looked at the dismayed little girl. "Go get your noodles and come eat with us. There's only cabbage soup tonight, but . . ."

"Oh, no," murmured Solange, "I already came over yesterday, and Tuesday . . ."

"But Mommie is asking you!" exclaimed Norette, drawing Soso farther into the room. "Let's get your noodles; I'll go with you!"

The two girls hurried out.

Madame Sellier put another bowl on the table and began to dish out the soup. Michel was already at his place, near Fanfan, who, sitting on a red cushion, followed with hungry eyes the movement of the soup ladle.

"I want more," he said when his mother had served him.

"First eat what you have, then we'll see about more; and try not to make such a mess. Here are the girls. Michel, bring another chair, and you Soso, let me have your noodles—I'll warm them with ours."

They all sat around the small table and ate their soup in silence. Norette kept turning her head and smiling at her friend, as if they had a secret between them. She was dark-complexioned and strong—a little heavy—with a willful chin and eyes of dark blue, almost purple. She had a determined manner. Michel resembled his sister but seemed more restless and unpredictable. His face changed expression every few moments, and one never knew what to expect from him next. That day he had a scratch on his cheek and his sweater was torn at the elbow.

"I see you've torn your sweater again," his mother remarked. "How did you manage it this time?"

Michel examined his sleeve as if he were seeing the tear for the first time. "Where? That? Wait, let me think. . . . Oh, yes, I remember now. That happened when we were playing 'invasion'—during the three-o'clock recess. Boy, did we surprise the Germans! They were the trees, in the playground—and we were the attackers. . . . Like this: bing, bang, bong!"

"And was it a 'tree' that tore your sleeve?" the mocking Norette wanted to know.

"No, smarty, of course not, but it was because some of us had to drown in the sea. So big Bobin had to rescue me, to drag me out of the water by the arm, and that was how . . . You see, so it was Bobin's fault, not mine!"

Madame Sellier sighed, "Nevertheless, all this means that I'll have one more thing to mend this evening. And if you continue to participate in daily 'invasions,' there'll soon be nothing left of your sweater. Can't you boys play at something else?"

"You know that they can't live without fighting," Norette said, talking like a grownup. "Boys can think of absolutely nothing else!"

"Is that so?" Michel said, making a face. "And girls—what do they play?"

Norette swallowed a big mouthful of noodles and answered with great seriousness, "This morning we played air-raid alert. That was a lot of fun, wasn't it, Soso?"

"Oh, yes!" Solange readily agreed, her sad little face brightening. "We took our 'children' down to the cellar. I had ten of them and Norette eight."

"And what did you use for children?" It was Michel's turn to be sarcastic.

"Pebbles."

"Oh, no-o-o! Peb . . . peb . . . bles!" Michel exploded with laughter. He laughed so hard that he choked on his food and began to cough, his nose buried in his napkin.

"And what about your 'trees'?" shrieked Norette. "There, you swallowed wrong! Serves you right! Serves you right!"

She nudged Solange with her elbow and the little girl smiled in agreement, while Fanfan observed the scene with indifference.

"Come on, children," urged Madame Sellier, "hurry up, finish your dinner, you little sillies. You see? What did I tell you? We're late. . . . Someone is knocking. . . . It must be the Moscots!"

Their neighbors came in, shivering. With them was their son George, a short, curly-haired boy, a classmate of Michel.

"Hi, there," Michel greeted them. "We haven't finished our dinner yet. George, do you want my noodles? I hate them!"

"Michel, offer your chair to Madame Moscot," his mother said. "Watch your manners instead of talking nonsense. And you, Norette, please help me clear off."

There were a few moments of confusion. Fanfan profited by it to gulp down the noodles his brother had left on his plate. After that, stuffed to the gills, he licked the plate.

"Are you finished *now,* you piglet?" his mother asked. Then, noticing that Solange was also busying herself, she said to her, "Are you helping me, too, Soso? That's a good girl! Please put the plates in the sink, my child. I'll wash them later." Then she gave her attention to the visitors. "Please have a seat, Madame Moscot."

The frail Madame Moscot sank into a chair. "How nice it is here," she sighed. "That stairway is frigid! You can catch your death of cold out there. What a winter this has been!"

"Yes," Madame Sellier agreed. Her mood changed noticeably as she added, "They must be miserable with the cold over there, in the prison camps. My husband doesn't mention it in his letters, since it's not allowed, but . . ."

"They say conditions are terrible over there, in Germany . . ." remarked Monsieur Moscot, a very tall, spare man. He stopped abruptly, noticing the warning in his wife's eyes.

"Don't listen to him, my dear," she said, trying to quiet Madame Sellier's anxiety. "My husband sees everything in black colors. Besides, this war's got to end sometime. . . . It just can't go on forever . . ." She tried to sound convincing, but her face begged for reassurance.

The Moscots were Jewish people, from Poland. Their real name was Moscowitz. They had left the French city of Lyons in July of 1942, at the time of mass arrests of Jews by the Germans, and had come to hide in Paris, under an assumed name. They were staying in an apartment which friends, now living in Orange, let them occupy. But they trembled with fear every time their bell rang. Madame Sellier looked at her neighbors in silence. They had even more to contend with, by far, than people like her, she thought. For they lived from morning to night in fear for their very lives. She composed herself and answered Madame Moscot in a convincing tone.

"Of course the war will end. . . . You'll see, next Christmas we'll all celebrate together. You just wait and see! We'll certainly make merry *that* day!"

"Do you really think so?" asked Monsieur Moscot doubtfully.

"I'm positive! Just think how far the Russians have advanced! But, excuse me a moment, I have to put Fanfan to bed. I'll be right back. Come along, Fanfan."

Fanfan objected a little, just out of habit, but his eyes were heavy with sleep and he let himself be taken off to bed without resisting. While the other children were finishing piling up the dishes, George drew Michel to one side.

"Well," he whispered, "have you finished?"

"Almost," Michel whispered back. "There were only two more copies left to do, but Mother interrupted and sent me out for some milk. . . . You know, it's going to be great! What a composition! No wonder they say you're the best one in the class in French."

George assumed a modest air, "Do you think it'll do?"

"You bet! It'll make an impression on the whole neighborhood!"

"Boys, what are you whispering about over there?" asked Norette.

Michel replied, "Oh, nothing. Anyway, things that are none of your business."

Madame Sellier now rejoined her visitors. "Fanfan is already asleep," she said. "He was dead tired. . . . Now, how about the broadcast? I wonder if we've missed it?"

She turned the knob and tuned in to the right station. They heard a great deal of static mixed with loud voices and lively jazz music. "They've invented a new kind of jamming," said Monsieur Moscot. "Are we going to be able to make anything out this evening?" He walked over to the radio and put his ear to it.

Through all the hubbub a distant voice was heard announcing, "This is London. Today, on this 1267th day of the struggle of the French people for their liberation, the French in exile are talking to their countrymen at home. . . ."

"Good!" said Madame Sellier, "they're just beginning the news. I guess my clock *is* fast."

The voice over the radio continued, sometimes drowned out by the jamming, sometimes clear: "The English have taken the offensive in southern Italy. General

Eisenhower has been named chief of all Anglo-American forces. West of Moscow, the Soviet troops are pressing on Vitebsk." Then the announcer reported on the exploits of the *maquisards*—the underground resisters inside France—during the past three months: one hundred and seventy-three train derailments; twenty-four ambushes of the enemy; a German detachment of sixty men decimated in Grenoble.

Solange, who had been leaning across the table absent-mindedly, started and asked anxiously, "What? What did they say? Did they say something about Grenoble?"

"About Grenoble?" said Madame Sellier. "Yes, they mentioned it. But why do you ask?"

Solange lifted her little thin face toward Madame Sellier, and her lips trembled as she answered, "It's because he's near there—Alain! He told me he was going to the mountains—Grenoble is in the mountains, isn't it? Oh, Madame Sellier, was he fighting against that German detachment?"

"Now, now," Madame Sellier comforted the little girl, hugging her. "Aren't you letting your imagination run away with you? There are lots of mountains, you know. What makes you think that your brother is exactly at that spot? Calm down, my dear, and try to be a brave little girl."

"Yes," murmured Solange, "I'll try . . ." and she bowed her head, trying not to cry.

Madame Moscot leaned toward Madame Sellier and whispered, "Poor mite! What a miserable life for so young a child—to have to worry about such things; to be alone, always alone, to have so little to eat, and to be always tormented by worry! I often wonder how she can sleep at night without being scared to death! How lucky for the little one that you are right across the hall!"

"I do all I can for her, of course. We have to help each other, don't we, since there's nothing else we can do."

"Yes. God forbid that she should end up getting sick from all the strain—just look at her! When I think of all the care I try to give my George . . ." and Madame Moscot looked tenderly at her son.

"Sh-h-h, listen!" Monsieur Moscot suddenly said, lifting his hand. The sound of the siren rose in the night. It pierced the silence, died down, wailed again.

"Another alert," sighed Madame Moscot. "What should we do?"

"I think we should all go down tonight," replied Madame Sellier, rising. "The headquarters of *their* Air Force are now in the Senate building. The building has become a strategic target. The English planes seem to concentrate on it. Last time the bombs fell quite close."

"You're right, all of us should go down," said Monsieur Moscot. "What a plague!" he added.

"Hurray!" cried Michel. "It's going to be fun down there in the shelter! We're going to have fun, aren't we George?"

"Yes, yes, but put your coats on," Madame Sellier reminded them. "I'm going to wake Fanfan. What a pity! —he's sleeping so soundly."

"And I'm going upstairs to get some warm clothes," said Madame Moscot. "Are you coming, Alfred?" The Moscots left.

The children went out into the hall. The sirens had stopped howling. The planes purred over the city. Then several thuds could be heard. A harsh voice shouted from the street, "For God's sake, put out your lights up there—on the fifth!"

"Where is Solange?" asked Norette. "And you, Michel, where are you going?" she said, noticing that her brother had opened the door to go back into the apartment.

"I left my coat in the dining room," he said. He soon returned to the hall, wearing his coat. He had slipped something wrapped in newspaper into it.

"You will break your neck in the dark, going down the stairs with that thing inside your coat," Norette warned. "You might as well just carry it under your arm."

"What thing? What do you mean by *it*?" growled Michel.

"You know—your box, that precious printing set of yours."

The boys looked at Norette with such openmouthed consternation that she burst out laughing. "Did you think I didn't guess anything? George, you ought to have watched Michel—you ought to have seen the fuss he made over that box, the trouble he took to hide it! I saw him shove it under the cupboard."

"All right, but you'd better shut up about it," the furious Michel advised her. He stopped abruptly; for his mother now appeared, carrying Fanfan.

"He didn't wake up," she said. "Are you ready? Let's go. Quickly! But where is Solange?"

"Here I am," said a small voice from behind her, and Solange appeared carrying her doll in her arms. The boys burst out laughing.

"Ha, ha, ha!" teased Michel. "You went to get your 'daughter,' one of the 'pebbles,' I suppose?"

"Leave her alone!" Madame Sellier urged gently. "Soso, come with me, dear."

Solange held on to Madame Sellier's dress with her free hand, and followed her timidly.

The Moscots were waiting for them on the lower landing, and the small company went down the stairs together, groping their way in the dark. Doors were being opened and shut throughout the house. People could be heard calling to one another, and above all others rose the shrill voice of the concierge—the building custodian—Madame Queline. "Hurry up, it's an air raid!" she was saying to everyone passing her door on the way down to the shelter.

There was a violent explosion, followed by the crackling of antiaircraft guns.

"What a bomb *that* was!" commented Monsieur Moscot knowingly. "Madame Sellier, be careful on that last step. Here we are, at last!"

They all crowded as best they could into the end of a narrow, dark passageway, which offered the greatest protection. Jean Morizot (he was usually called Monsieur Jean), the first-floor tenant, had brought along a candle which he placed on a wooden box. He was sitting on another box, alongside a robust, graying man whom everyone called Grandfather Lampion. The elderly man lived on the ground floor. Seeing the new arrivals, he got up to give his place to Madame Sellier.

"They're coming down hard," he said in his deep voice. "It reminds me of the Battle of Ardennes, in 1917."

"Not a very pleasant memory, I'd say!" muttered Monsieur Jean, as he kept smoothing his blond hair fastidiously. "They make me sick to my stomach, those sirens! Why can't the English leave us in peace?"

Madame Queline looked at him askance. Two months ago her son had gotten through to Spain, and had later rejoined the French Army in Africa. The woman had since become very militant. "If everyone felt the way you do, we'd be in a fine fix!" she said. "I'm glad my boy isn't of your opinion. . . . Tell me, don't you want us to keep fighting against Hitler?"

"Yes, yes, of course . . . Hitler is a monster!" grumbled Monsieur Jean, now feeling somewhat ashamed. "But those things, the alerts . . . that's no way to live . . . to say nothing of the freezing temperature in my room and that . . . and that . . ." He searched for other proof of the horrible conditions under which everyone indeed lived, stammered, and, too frustrated to go on, adjusted his tie instead.

Michel regarded Monsieur Jean with puzzlement. The man was wrong, no doubt about it. But despite everything, he impressed Michel: after all, Monsieur Jean worked at a drugstore and, besides, he was always very well dressed. "What do *you* think?" he asked George in a whisper.

George sneered loudly. "He's nothing but a coward! He talks like that because he's afraid of the bombs. I bet when he was small he took all the beatings at school without fighting back." Then, changing the subject, George asked his friend, "Hey, why weren't you more careful with that printing set? Now your sister knows everything! What if she talks about it in front of Stéphane, even if she doesn't go into detail . . . We might all go to prison if that dirty spy gets suspicious!"

Michel looked at George, his mouth hanging open. He hadn't thought of that. Stéphane was their classmate. He was the elder son of the Gourres, owners of a paint store on the block and the tenants in the second-floor apartment. Stéphane's parents did business with the Germans, and it was rumored that they had made millions selling things to them. They often entertained a German officer in their home, and they were always well supplied with legs of mutton, sausages, and fresh eggs for him and for themselves. They were "the shame of the house," the concierge would often say. She avenged herself on these traitors by taking the mail up to them three days after the postman delivered it. Stéphane and Louis, their two sons, snooped around, eavesdropped at doors, and assumed an arrogant air when they were discovered. Everyone pretended not to notice the Gourres, as if they didn't exist. A conspiracy of silence surrounded them.

Michel finally roused himself from the effect of George's warnings about Stéphane's spying. "Don't you think," he said, "that Norette is too smart to do anything so silly? Anyway, I think she's bluffing, like all girls. I'm sure she knows nothing about what we're doing. She suspects we have a secret and she's trying to trick us into telling her about it. . . . I know her!" And Michel cast a superior look toward his sister, who, squatting on a box, was playing with Solange's doll.

Norette caught his glance. She blushed. "I bet the boys are laughing at me because of your doll," she said to Solange. "Maybe they think that I admire her. Not that she's *that* beautiful—your one-eyed wonder! Why couldn't you have left her upstairs!"

"Oh, is that so! And what if she got hit by a bomb?"

Solange said angrily, "What if she died? What would I do without her? You . . . you have Fanfan, and that's almost like having a doll, but I . . . I have no one. To whom would I talk when I was alone? And if you think Mimi's so ugly, then give her back to me!" And Solange indignantly pulled so hard at her doll that its little arm came off at the shoulder.

Solange started to cry. "What's the matter?" asked Madame Sellier, turning around. Seeing the loose arm, she smiled reassuringly. "That's nothing, Soso, give me your doll later and I'll mend her arm, at the same time that I sew up Michel's sweater. Come, don't cry. Use your hankie—your nose is running. If you don't have one, take mine. . . . There it is, in my pocket. I don't dare move because of Fanfan."

Solange took Madame Sellier's handkerchief, wiped her tears, and cuddled up against the shoulder of her protectress.

Old man Lampion who had gone outside "to look around," now came back, dragging his feet which were stiff with the cold. "It's coming down worse than ever," he reported. "What rotten luck! I must get a good night's sleep if I'm to be at the printing shop at seven in the morning. Come what may, I think I'll go upstairs and lie down."

The concierge raised her long, emaciated face and said to him urgently, "No, my man, you stay here! Once you came down, stay down! It's enough that the two Minet sisters refuse to budge out of their apartment during raids. I banged and banged at their door, but they insist on dying in their bed, as they say, and you may be sure that's where they are now, with the sheets pulled up around their chins. If they're hit, so much the worse for them! No one can say I didn't warn them!"

"You know," joked old man Lampion, "there's some sense to their staying up there—at least they'll get a good night's sleep . . . even if it may be a longer sleep than they bargained for. . . ."

He yawned loudly, then stopped abruptly in the middle of a second yawn, saying, "I wonder who is coming down now? That wouldn't be your Minet ladies after all, would it, Madame Queline?"

It was not the spinster sisters. It was the Gourre family, each and every one of them, plus chairs and picnic baskets. The father and the two sons, all three fat and redheaded, were muffled up in heavy, fur-collared jackets. The mother wore a squirrel fur coat which made her look like a shaggy bear.

"We could have managed very well without them," Monsieur Moscot muttered. He withdrew apprehensively to the darker recess of the shelter, his eyes resting anxiously on George. Silence fell on the gathering, broken only by the scraping of the chairs that the Gourres were setting up along the passageway.

"Put them farther down, Stéphane," Madame Gourre was saying in a voice like a trumpet. "You know it's less safe in the front here—the *others* can move together a bit."

But the *others* stubbornly refused to budge. What's more, they suddenly seemed to have become deaf and dumb. Madame Queline sat staring into space; Monsieur Jean pulled a book from his pocket and was pretending to read, although he couldn't see a thing; old man Lampion kept blowing his nose laboriously, and Madame

Sellier, freeing one of her arms, hugged Solange to her.

Madame Gourre's lips tightened. "Stéphane, did you hear what I said?" she snapped.

"Gosh," Stéphane grumbled, "where do you expect me to put your chairs? Can't you see there's no room!"

"There is so—I'll show you!" Madame Gourre pushed the four chairs so close against the boxes on which the others were sitting that when she sat down her knees touched the concierge's.

"Look here, watch what you're doing!" Madame Queline said sharply, without deigning to look at the other woman.

"*You* watch out—all you have to do is move a little!" Madame Gourre snapped back.

"Now, now," her husband interceded in the tone of peacemaker, "don't upset yourself, Berthe. . . . What a night," he added, "and all this on account of those accursed English! What a swarm of planes they sent over tonight! They're sure trying to help their French *friends!*"

"Good thing that the Germans have such a superior air-raid defense," said his wife. "If they shoot down enough of them, I . . ."

A trumpetlike blast drowned out her voice. It was old man Lampion blowing his nose again. And, at once, as if by signal, handkerchiefs were pulled out of pockets and all the tenants began to blow their noses, making a great din.

"I . . ." repeated Madame Gourre, trying to finish her sentence. This time everyone was seized by violent fits of coughing. Coughing, sneezing, and sniffling filled the shelter. Fanfan woke up and began to shout with all his might, "Three cheers for the bombs!"

Madame Gourre gave up trying to make herself heard and vented her frustration on her sons. "Sit up properly," she yelled at them. "Louis, stop scratching yourself!"

"I'm hungry," Louis whimpered.

"Me, too," said the father. "Come, Mama, let's have some food!"

Madame Gourre opened her basket and got out several thick sandwiches. A delicious smell of pork sausage filled the shelter. The cacophony ceased and everyone sniffed the good smell, which they had almost forgotten over the past three years.

"Look at those two kids stuffing themselves," whispered Madame Moscot in her husband's ear.

"Darn it, it makes me hungry to look at them and their sandwiches. Odette, you should have brought down something, too," said Monsieur Moscot.

"What, for heaven's sake, the rest of the turnips?"

Stéphane now left his chair, sandwich in hand, and walked over to Michel. His heavy jacket, much too long for him, trailed down to his calves. "Hi there," he said, his mouth full. And without waiting to be greeted in turn, he continued, "Did you do your problems for tomorrow?"

Michel whistled to himself and looked at George, who tried not to laugh.

"Did you do the problems?" Stéphane persisted. "The one about the trains—did you do that one?"

Michel at last turned toward him, as if he had just discovered his presence. "The problem?" he said, stretching out the words. "The problem about the trains? . . ."

"Yes, you know, there were two of them."

"Two problems?" Michel kept up the pretense of not knowing what Stéphane was talking about. "Oh, *those* two problems! Have you done those two, George?"

"The two problems? Let me see," George mused. "The two problems . . . two problems . . ."

The two friends winked at each other and whistled a duet. Stéphane, furious, reddened under his freckles. "I know you don't want to answer me, but I don't care. I don't give a damn!"

Michel said, "Then why did you bother to ask us?"

"Well, I mean that . . . Say, what do you have there, inside your coat? Show it to me. It's pretty bulky!"

Before Michel had a chance to stop him, Stéphane grabbed the box. The paper in which it was wrapped tore, exposing the lid of the printing set.

"'The Little Printer,'" Stéphane read. "So, you're a printer now? And what do you print? Can I see?"

George grew pale. Michel bit his lip nervously.

"Give it back to me, you idiot!" he cried, throwing himself at Stéphane.

Stéphane shook him off, but, hampered by his sandwhich, he let the box drop from his hands. The string came undone and small pieces of green paper flew in all directions.

Michel screamed, "George! Norette! Help me!"

George and Norette rushed over. Louis threw himself into the fray to help his brother. The five children groped about on their hands and knees in the semidark for the papers. Every time a Gourre seized one, the others snatched it out of his hand. Their cries mingled with the calls of the Moscots and the booming voice of Madame Gourre, who was shouting:

"Leave my boys alone, you good-for-nothings!"

At last the turmoil subsided, and when the combatants rose from the ground, smeared with dust and soot, the victory was clearly on Michel's side—the two Gourres hadn't retained a single scrap of paper.

"I must say, I'm not proud of you!" Madame Sellier said softly. "You've put on quite a show!"

"It was Stéphane's fault," said Michel, out of breath. "He . . ."

"You little liar," shrieked Madame Gourre. "It was *you* who threw yourself on *him.* I saw it with my own two eyes!"

"But he took my box!" Michel defended himself, not looking at the woman.

"You liar! You liar!" Madame Gourre kept repeating, brandishing her sandwich in the air.

A blast of old man Lampion's "trumpet" answered her, and everybody returned to his seat, as if nothing had happened. Madame Gourre, still fuming, wrapped herself grandly in her fur and called her sons to her side. Louis obeyed her, but Stéphane continued to hang around Michel.

Grinning maliciously, he said, "I know what those papers are. They are political leaflets."

Michel flinched, "Leaflets? You're crazy! Did you hear him, George?"

"What an imbecile!" George said. "An utter imbecile!"

It was obvious that George didn't know what else to say. Stéphane looked him up and down.

"They *are* leaflets," he gloated. "They are leaflets against the Germans!"

Norette, who until then had been listening in silence, now briskly took a piece of paper from her pocket. It was green, exactly like the others. She held it up between her fingers.

"Norette!" Michel screamed. "What . . . what are you doing?"

"Let me! I'm sick and tired of all this talk about leaflets." Then, turning to Stéphane, she asked, "If I show you this paper, then will you believe us?"

"I . . . yes," said Stéphane, his eyes glued to the green paper.

She held it out to Stéphane. "Here it is. Let me show it to him," she said to Michel and George, who had darted toward her. "It's not a secret."

The two boys stared at Norette, baffled. Stéphane took advantage of the pause to grab the paper from her hand. He took it quickly to the light of the candle.

The more he read the longer his face became. He finally returned the green scrap to Norette, making no comment.

"Are you satisfied now?" Norette asked mockingly.

"All right," Stéphane mumbled; then, turning to his mother, he said sullenly, "Mom, I'm still hungry."

Just as his mother was hurriedly reaching into the basket for another sandwich, the siren blared, announcing the end of the raid.

"At last!" exclaimed the concierge.

There was a general bustle, everyone stretching to get rid of the numbness. They gathered up their things and started climbing the house stairs, yawning.

"We gave those collaborators a real rough time, didn't we?" whispered old man Lampion as he was opening the door to his place. "My nose is sore from blowing it so hard, but it was worth it. . . . Well, good night everybody."

Michel was barely inside their apartment when he rushed over to Norette. "Gee, you scared me! I thought you gave Stéphane a . . . real leaflet! What did you show him?"

In reply Norette handed her piece of green paper to Michel. He read the following, poorly printed, lines:

> What *thing* dances? – The flame.
> What *thing* sleeps? – The water in the fishpond.
> What *thing* snores? – The wood stove.
> What *thing* falls? – The night.

"How . . . how did you do this?" Michel stammered.

Norette giggled. "Well, I'll tell you–you really got on my nerves with your mysterious box. So I got hold of it to see what you were so anxious to hide–that day you had hidden the box in the hamper–and then I had fun printing these riddles. Wasn't it lucky that I had them with me tonight? I took them along to the shelter to show Solange. Don't you think I made a big monkey out of Stéphane Gourre? Did you see his face? He certainly didn't expect to find this sort of thing printed on the green paper."

"You're right," Michel agreed. "However, you had no business stealing my printing set."

"But it did get you out of trouble, didn't it? Didn't I get you out of a jam?"

"Hmm . . . yes. . . ."

Norette looked at him, her usually cool eyes gleaming with mischief. "Well, then what are you complaining about?" she said, having the last word. "I'm sleepy. I'm going to bed," she announced casually, and quickly walked out of the room, head high, before her brother had time to answer her.

The Pirates of the Résistance

Next day Michel woke up in a bad mood. He was still sleepy because he had gone to bed late. Also, he was angry with Norette. She had gotten him out of trouble, true, but she had discovered his secret as well. Besides, he was annoyed because he had been outsmarted by a girl. And where could he hide his printing set from her? He now removed the green sheets of paper from it and stuffed them in his pockets. Then, after thinking for a brief moment, he hid the box on the grocery shelf in the kitchen, behind the package of noodles. Since the family had just had noodles yesterday, he figured that his mother would not touch the package for another few days. Meanwhile, he would have time to think of a better hiding place. He now felt better, downed his cup of artificial coffee made from roasted barley, and raced upstairs to call for George.

But George was still asleep. His mother explained, speaking in a whisper, that the late alert had worn him out and that he would not be going to school that morning. "What a sissy!" Michel thought. "They certainly coddle him!" He raced down the house stairs, four at a time, plunged into the street, and walked toward Rue Monsieur-le-Prince, his book bag under his arm.

A column of German soldiers was marching up the street, chanting their sinister songs to the slow staccato rhythm of their steps. An officer was goose-stepping at the head. He looked so squeezed into his tight uniform and held himself so rigidly that he seemed to have swallowed a ramrod. As he was passing where Michel stood watching, he slipped on the hard snow and went sprawling on the pavement.

"*Ach!*" he growled. "*Donnerwetter!*" (Thunderation!)

Michel looked at him from the corner of his eye, then past him, saying to himself, "Serves you right, you damn Nazi, serves you right! It's too bad you didn't drop dead like the others!" The "others" had been a detachment of Germans who had been attacked two months before, right on that very spot, by a group of *francs-tireurs*, soldiers of the French underground army. Norette, who had at that moment come out of the bakery, saw the Germans flee like madmen as they were being pelted with hand grenades. They kept firing their rifles wildly as they fled. They fired at anything, at walls, windows. The inhabitants of the house had enjoyed the sight in silence. Although they were "occupied" by the Nazis, no one could stop them from thinking whatever they wanted to —and wasn't that really what it meant to be free? . . .

"That's some sight!" murmured Michel as, on the sly, he watched the German officer rise clumsily from the ground. "Wait till I tell the boys about this," he mused. "What will big Bobin say when I tell him that I saw a

German sprawled in the gutter, his arms and legs in the air—Bobin who had made such a big thing out of merely seeing a Nazi lose his cap on a windy day? A German taking a flop is certainly a much prettier sight than a German chasing his cap!" Michel continued on his way to school, feeling all cheered up.

As he turned into Rue de Vaugirard, a tall man greeted him. It was Monsieur Planquet, the carpenter from Rue de l'Estrapade, for whom Michel's father had worked before the war.

"Hello, son," the man said in his hoarse voice. "What news from the prisoner?"

"I don't know, monsieur," Michel answered, taking off his beret. "Father hasn't written for some time, but Mother sent him a nice parcel for Christmas. And I contributed my chocolate ration," he added, not concealing his pride.

"That was a nice thing to do. And how is school? Are you getting good grades?"

"Only average, Monsieur Planquet. It's those problems, you know . . ." he said vaguely.

"Good, good . . . so long, my little man. Drop by to see me one of these days," the carpenter said absently, and he went on his way.

Michel followed him with his eyes and replaced the beret on his head. He greatly admired Monsieur Planquet, first of all because he was so tall, then because he had in his shop a most extraordinary carpenter's plane. It was enormous, probably the biggest in the world, he thought. When his father used it in the past, the looped shavings flew as if a gust of wind were scattering them. Michel would gather up the longest ones and make sailboats out of them, which he sent floating down the little stream running along the gutter. The "boats" floated, stopped, floated again, and were suddenly swallowed up by the sewer opening.

"Yes, I'll go to see him," Michel planned happily. "Maybe he'll let me have some of those shavings. . . . But, wow! it's eight-forty, and I'm late!" He quickened his pace.

The class was already in session when Michel got to school. Monsieur Touron, a little man as round as his name, with a red face and thick lips, was about to call Stéphane Gourre to the blackboard. Michel quickly slipped into his seat, between Mourette and Gilles Ménard. But Monsieur Touron had a sharp eye.

"Late again, Sellier," he scolded. "It's the second time this week, my boy!"

"Yes, monsieur, it's because I met someone on the way. . . . Also, it's because of the air raid; Mother insisted that I go down to the shelter, so, this morning I . . . I didn't wake up in time."

"But," remarked the teacher, "you're not the only one. Who else went down to a shelter yesterday evening?" he asked the class.

The whole class stirred and many hands were raised, and Stéphane, now standing at the blackboard, a piece of chalk in his hand, waved his hand harder than anyone else. "Me, monsieur, me!" he yelled.

"You see?" said Monsieur Touron when calm was restored. "Try to remember to set your alarm clock ahead a bit, lazybones! Now, enough talk, let's return to our problems. Gourre, what is your answer?"

Stéphane's face fell. He scribbled several numbers,

erased them with his finger, ran his hand through his mop of red hair, and blinked.

"Well, is that all?" asked the teacher.

"No, monsieur, but . . . I can't remember . . . but it's all in my notebook. . . ."

"In your notebook? Look here, it should be in your head as well. Go back to your seat. Moscot! . . . Let's see, where is Moscot?"

"He's absent," several voices informed him.

"Because of the air raid," added Michel. "He . . ."

Monsieur Touron looked crossly at him. "The air raid? Again? Can't you think of anything else but the air raid?"

"Yes . . . no . . . monsieur, but I went up to get him, and his mother said he was tired and that . . ."

"All right, that'll do. Barroux, you go to the board."

Tiny Barroux, blond and pale, took the piece of chalk from Stéphane and wrote down the figures in the problem. His writing was large and precise. Michel stared at the column of numbers without actually seeing them. He had just remembered that he hadn't had time yesterday evening to finish solving the second problem. If only Monsieur Touron didn't call on him! "After all," he reasoned, "there is only one chance in thirty-eight of being called on, since there are thirty-nine in the class." He sat up very properly on his bench and tried to look as inconspicuous as possible. Barroux wrote down the last figure, underlining it carefully because it was the answer to the problem.

"Good!" said the teacher. "Now, it's your turn Sellier; let's have the second problem."

Michel rose slowly. "It's because . . . because . . ."

"Well, because what?"

"It's because of the air raid, monsieur; I had planned to do it after dinner, it . . . the air raid . . ."

The class tittered. Monsieur Touron rapped on his desk.

"See here, Sellier, are you trying to make a fool of me with that air raid of yours!"

"But, Monsieur Touron, it's true, I assure you," stammered Michel, blushing up to his ears. "I assure you it's absolutely true this time!"

"What do you mean 'this time'? How about the other times—you didn't tell the truth? Very well, this will earn you a nice round zero, my friend, and *that* at least is true!"

Michel sat down with as much dignity as he could manage under the circumstances, since all around him he could hear jeering voices whispering in a singsong, "Air raid, air raid, air raid!"

"You morons!" he hissed.

Ménard nudged him with his elbow. "Pay no attention. . . . Say, do you have *them*?"

"Yes."

Michel no longer thought of his bad grade. What did a zero matter, or trains in an arithmetic problem, when one was, like himself, a combatant against the enemy? He now waited on pins and needles for the lesson to end. As soon as the recess bell rang, he dashed outside with all the others.

"What do we play today?" cried Mourette. "'Invasion,' like yesterday?"

"Oh no!" objected Roche, a thin little boy with a turned-up nose. "I've had enough of 'invasion.' Bobin always gets to be the officer."

Big Bobin gave him an annihilating look. "What do you expect?" he said. "Someone has to be in command, and is it my fault that I'm the only one here who knows how to *spikingliche?*"

"Spikingliche, spikingliche!" Roche mimicked him, choking with laughter. "As to spikingliche, old man, you can't say anything except '*Hullow boys!*' Just that one thing, that's all. You're nothing but a show-off!"

"What about you?" retorted Bobin, hurt to the quick.

"Me? Just listen to this: '*Good morning, sir, the cat is on the moon; it's a long way to Tipperary.*' Well, what do you think of that?"

Bobin shrugged his shoulders. "That's not English, that's gibberish which you made up!"

"I made up? What nerve! My cousin taught it to me, and it *is* English, English, English!"

"Liar!"

"You're a liar yourself! You call me liar because you didn't understand what I said and you don't dare admit it. If you're so smart, tell me what it means—'the cat is on the moon'?"

Bobin was silent. All eyes were on him, filled with doubt. He felt he had to restore his prestige somehow. "I don't give a hang!" he declared. "So much the worse for all of you! No more 'invasion!' Let's play air raid instead. At least that should please Sellier!"

At once all the doubters and sneerers went over to Bobin's side. "That's right," they cried, "the famous air raid that kept him from doing so many things!"

"Well, are we going to start?" asked Bobin, vindicated.

Michel made a face. "Leave me out," he said sourly. "I don't play girls' games! . . . Are some of you fellows

coming with me?" he added in a meaningful tone, saying this without looking at anyone in particular. However, Ménard, Roche, Mourette, and little Barroux at once separated from the rest of the boys and followed Michel, smiling mysteriously.

"What a phony!" Bobin burst out, beside himself with rage. "Who does that Sellier think he is—him and his *complot*, his secret plans?"

"He must think he is the *generalissimo* or something!" said a dark-skinned little fellow, puffing with laughter.

Stéphane walked over to Bobin and asked with sly curiosity, "What is that *complot* you're talking about?"

The dark-skinned boy abruptly stopped laughing, and Bobin looked down at his feet, saying, "You're imagining things, no one said anything about any complot."

"Yes, you did, you're the one who said it. . . ."

"I said . . . I said . . . Oh! I remember now, I said *compo*—you know, short for *composition*, the one that Sellier wrote, the one for which he got the second-best grade! What did you think I said, stupid?"

Stéphane didn't insist. He never insisted when he felt he was the loser.

"Br-r-r." He shivered with the cold. "I'm freezing! Who wants to play tag?" he asked.

In the meantime, the five "conspirators" were approaching the bicycle-parking area at the end of the schoolyard, behind the lime trees. Michel stopped to recover his breath, "Phew! Here we are at last! Come on, fellows, hurry up! I have the leaflets!" He reached into his pockets feverishly and brought out a handful of small green sheets of paper.

"What a lot of them!" exclaimed Roche, his eyes like saucers.

"You said it!" said Michel, puffed up with pride. "There are sixty of them. And did it ever take a long time to print them!—that, by the way, was the real reason I didn't do my problem!"

"Poor Michel," commiserated little Barroux. "And Touron gave you a zero!"

"Who cares? Duty before all else! And guess who wrote the text? It was Moscot. Wait till you see how well it's written! Listen to this!" Michel coughed to clear his throat and read, declaiming a bit:

Pirates of the Résistance

Great League of France for Liberty

People of Paris, the hour of Liberation is near! The English planes fly over France almost daily, the Russians are advancing toward Germany, and the Germans are beginning to be very scared, although they don't want to show it. Be ready for the revolt, support our League, join the Pirates of the Résistance. They will achieve magnificent things. They will not shirk anything that would make them worthy of marching under the Arch of Triumph when the Day of Glory is here.

Long Live Liberty! Long Live the Pirates!

LONG LIVE FRANCE!

"See, isn't it great?"

The four boys were spellbound with admiration.

"That's wonderful!" Roche finally said in a voice full

of rapture. "And . . . do you really think we'll march under the Arch of Triumph? Do you really think so?"

"Of course! Those who were in the thick of it—they'll have the honor! Can't you just see the six of us marching in the parade?"

"Yes, yes," said Ménard in his usual calm voice, "but there's something you've overlooked. The leaflet says: 'Support our League.' How can people support it if they don't know our address?"

"You are right," Michel said, embarrassed. "I didn't think of that. What do we do now? Well, suppose we see about that when we do the next leaflet. The important thing at first is to influence opinion, and we *are* influencing opinion, aren't we, men? Now, let's see: there are sixty leaflets, and there are six of us—that makes it exactly ten for each one. Here, take yours. I'll keep Moscot's."

Avid hands were stretched toward Michel.

"You put only one 't' in 'Pirates,'" Ménard pointed out.

"One is enough."

"No, there should be two."

"Do you think so? Oh nuts!—the spelling doesn't matter. What matters is how to distribute these. I thought of it last night; we must stick them in the mailboxes, the ones for the letter carriers, and . . . and . . . anywhere else we can."

"Too bad we can't scatter them from a high window," said fat Mourette excitedly. "That would make a big impression. . . . I happen to live on the fourth floor."

Michel looked at him scornfully. "That's right," he scoffed, "so that your house may be surrounded and searched. . . . Do you think you are in *The Three Musketeers?* This is for real, not a game!"

Mourette lowered his face, mortified.

"I've thought of something else," announced Ménard. "We've got to change our names. Everyone does it in the Résistance!"

"Yes! Yes! Let's!" Roche and Barroux cried.

"That's a great idea!" Michel said solemnly. "I've already decided on mine—I'm going to call myself *Hercules.*"

"And I, *Maximilian,* like Robespierre," said Ménard. Roche chose *Caesar* and Barroux *Donald,* in honor of Walt Disney's hero. As for Mourette, he said he had chosen the name *Bouc.*

"Bouc!" the others guffawed. "Why Bouc? What a ridiculous name—'Bouc'!" But Mourette remained resolute. He absolutely insisted on Bouc.

"Very well, let it be Bouc," Michel gave in.

"Let it be Bouc!" the mocking voices of the rest repeated after him.

Just then the other gang, with Bobin in the lead, descended on the bicycle-parking area.

"Quick, hide the leaflets!" Michel whispered. The green papers disappeared into pockets.

"Well," cried Bobin, "are you through with all your nonsense? Whose name is Bouc? Is it Mourette's?"

"What do you care? It doesn't matter, anyhow," answered Roche. "We're only playing!"

"They're playing 'riddles,'" explained Stéphane mockingly. "Hey, Sellier, is the answer to your sister's riddle *Bouc?*—the riddle she showed me yesterday in the shelter?" And he looked intently at Michel, scratching his head hard.

"No one can hide anything from you, can they?"

Michel said contemptuously. "Anyway, we are finished playing this game. Now let's all play *balle au chasseur* —playing tag will warm us up."

Michel took his handkerchief out of his pocket and rolled it into a ball. The boys scattered to avoid being touched. Bobin, in passing, purposely brushed against Michel. "Be careful of Gourre!" he whispered.

Michel winked to signal that he understood what Bobin had meant, then, taking advantage of his proximity, he threw the handkerchief right at him. "It touched you, you are *it!*"

Bobin picked up the handkerchief, and the game continued, with everyone shrieking something or other.

Little Barroux, who did not like to play running games, hid behind a lime tree. Suddenly someone touched him on the shoulder. It was Stéphane. "I want to tell you something. Let's go to the bicycle shed." He pulled Barroux toward the shed and kept talking. The small boy tried to shake him off but the other was stronger than he.

"What do you want from me?" he asked, frightened.

"How would you like me to give you a good beating?"

Barroux cast a desperate glance in the direction of Michel and Ménard, who were busy chasing each other at the other end of the yard. "N . . . no," he stammered. "No, of course not. . . ."

"Then give me the papers you are hiding in your pocket—the green ones."

"What . . . what papers? I have no papers!"

"Yes, you have so! Listen, if you'll give me just one of them, then not only will you get no beating but instead I'll bring you a chocolate. A real one. Even two. You'll love them!"

Barroux stared at him. "I don't know what you want," he cried shrilly, "and I have no papers, not one!"

"Is that so? We'll see!" Stéphane threatened, and pinning back one of the small boy's arms, he began to rummage in his pockets.

Barroux, gritting his teeth, tried to push him away. "Let go of me!" he shrieked. His cries finally reached Michel and he came running, the handkerchief ball in his hand.

"Let him go!" he snapped at Stéphane. "What do you want with him?"

"Oh, nothing," said Stéphane, grinning maliciously.

He let go of Barroux's arm, continued to grin but said nothing. Barroux looked straight at Michel and when their eyes met, he said:

"He wants some kind of papers—green ones. He promised to give me chocolate."

"I wanted those riddles," Stéphane lied casually. "I wanted to take a look at them, to see if they were funny. Now, that's not against the law, is it?" He kept grinning, to look innocent. Michel wasn't fooled.

"You rotten spy!" he said, gritting his teeth. "Don't think we don't know what you're looking for!"

Stéphane flushed a beet red. He stopped smiling.

"Now I'm a 'spy'!" he cried. "What next! You make me sick, all of you! You're all crazy, with your leaflets and all that claptrap! My dad's right, he calls it 'claptrap.'"

"So," said Michel, "your dad . . ."

"And what about yours? He's a prisoner! He certainly has nothing to be proud of! The loser!"

Stéphane fell silent, afraid that he had gone too far,

but since no one said anything, he began to grin again, sheepishly.

His classmates stared him down. They felt instinctively that Stéphane's remarks were especially vile. It wasn't enough to answer him in kind. They were choking with indignation.

Suddenly Michel sprang at Stéphane and let go with a punch at his chest. The blow was so violent that his adversary fell, legs flying up into the air. Stéphane attempted to rise, but Michel grabbed him hard. The two rolled on the ground. That was quite a fight! The enemies were of equal strength, but Michel was quicker and more agile; Stéphane was heavier. They fought in silence, and the others were also silent as they watched the two with breathless excitement. Only little Barroux kept crying out, "Beat him, Sellier!" Everyone realized that Barroux was right, that Michel had to be the victor. Michel had Stéphane flat on his back and was pinning his shoulders to the ground when he heard the voice of Monsieur Touron behind him.

"What's going on here?"

The children remained rooted to the spot. The teacher quickly cleared the way for himself, stopping in front of the combatants, who were still in each other's grip.

"Fine! My congratulations! You'll each get a zero in conduct, my friends! Now, let's go. Everybody back to class. In proper order, please."

The boys fell in line. Michel stopped for an instant to straighten his sweater, which now had a new tear—in the back.

The teacher came over and put his arm around his shoulder. "Sellier," he said, "I gave you a zero, and you deserved it, but I understand how it is. . . . Now, listen to me. I know that your father isn't home, and I'd like to talk to you, man to man. You're about to do something very foolish, young man! Believe me, you mustn't play around with that sort of thing . . . the leaflets."

"But, monsieur, I don't play around with them! . . ."

"Yes, you do, even if you don't realize it. You shouldn't do it. What you *should* do is work, and as hard as you can. I'm sure this is what your father would say to you even in times like these. Do you understand what I'm saying? . . . Next week be sure to do your problems."

"Yes, monsieur."

"Go along now, Sellier. Join your classmates, young man."

Michel caught up with the others, his heart beating fast. Everything was buzzing in his head. Later he couldn't listen to a single word of the history lesson, nor of the lesson in French, which followed. And when the lunch bell rang at ten-thirty, he ran home without waiting for the others.

"My teacher spoke to me," he kept repeating to himself. "He spoke to me, *man to man!*" Michel felt both proud and hurt—proud because he had not been treated like a child and had been spoken to seriously; hurt by what Monsieur Touron had said about his league. "How did he guess about the Pirates?" Michel wondered, somewhat bitterly. But, just the same, he was filled with pride. And with each step, his teacher assumed greater and greater importance. At the corner of Rue Monsieur-le-Prince, Michel admired him; then, as he was crossing Place de l'Odéon, he adored him. Yes, he vowed, from now on he'd do all his problems! From now on he'd get the best grades for all his homework. He'd prove to Monsieur Touron that he *was* a man!

At the height of this exaltation he even considered, but only for a moment, tearing up the green leaflets. He realized, however, that that would mean failing his comrades. He compromised by dropping his batch into the first mailbox he saw along the way. After which, feeling relieved, he turned into his street, the Rue des Quatre-Vents. At that moment he suddenly remembered the fight with Stéphane and the two zeros! As for the fight, it was a good thing, a real little victory over that Gourre, and, considering what that sneak was really after, a *great* victory! There remained the two zeros. What was he going to tell his mother? His father would have boxed his ears, for sure! As for his mother, he guessed he could always manage to get around her if he proceeded carefully. He did some rehearsing while climbing the stairs. Should he assume a dramatic air, or a sad one, or, perhaps, a defiant one? He decided to seem casual, with just a touch of sadness, and boldly entered the apartment.

His mother was on her knees, washing the tile floor in the kitchen.

"Mother . . ." he began. She raised her head, startled, and Michel noticed that she had been crying.

"How come you are crying?" he asked bluntly, and there was a tinge of reproach in his voice.

She wiped her eyes on her apron, trying to hide her emotion, as if she had been discovered doing something wrong. "Oh, it's nothing," she said. "It's just that everything went wrong this morning. Fanfan has a cold—he must have caught a chill last night, in the shelter. I hope it won't be anything serious. . . . He's been so frail since his ear infection. And I was going to give him some milk, but the milk we got yesterday had turned sour, and they told me at the dairy that they don't expect to have any today. Then . . . I am so exhausted!"

"Really?" asked Michel, and he added, somewhat reluctantly, "Would you like me to set the table?"

"If you want to."

"That's great!" thought Michel, disappointed. "And what about Norette?" he fumed inwardly, "taking it easy, I suppose?"

"And Norette?" he couldn't resist asking out loud.

His mother had resumed scrubbing the floor, and answered him without straightening up, "Norette is taking care of Fanfan, dear. . . . Did everything go well at school? Did you get good grades?"

Michel hesitated for a moment. Nothing was going the way he had planned it, and he felt a little annoyed with his mother because of it.

"I got two zeros," he said crossly, "and I tore my sweater. . . . Look!" He turned around to show the damage.

"Oh, again!" sighed Madame Sellier. "And I mended your sleeve only yesterday evening! How did you tear it today? And those zeros—that's no good, Michel."

"But it wasn't my fault, it was . . ."

"Now, now, don't shout; you'll upset your little brother. Go on, set the table; lunch is almost ready."

Michel obeyed. Wouldn't they even let him speak anymore? he complained to himself. Mother could at least have listened to him! He opened the cupboard noisily. Which plates was he supposed to use—the flat ones or the soup plates? He'd ask Norette. And he burst into his mother's room where Fanfan had his little bed and where Norette was now leaning over him, feeding him lime-blossom tea.

"What plates should I use?" he blurted out.

Norette turned around, cup in hand. "The flat ones," she said. "But why are you shouting that way? And what stories were you telling Mother, in the kitchen?"

"Stories? What stories? . . . I've told her nothing, although I have plenty to tell! Got two zeros, and had a fight with Stéphane. I knocked him down flat—you should have seen me! You know what he said? . . . He said that I shouldn't be proud of having a prisoner for a father, and he spoke to me like to some kind of defeated weakling. . . ." Then, pride taking hold of him, he added, "Wait till Mother hears about how I won that fight—boy! Will she be sorry that she didn't let me tell her before!"

Norette put down the half-full cup on the bedside table. "I'd like to give you some advice," she said calmly. "Don't you go and tell Mother anything at all about Stéphane."

"You don't say! And why not?"

"Because it will make her cry some more—it'll frighten her."

"Frighten her? Nonsense!"

"Do you think so? Don't you understand *anything*? Don't you understand how dangerous the Gourres are? Mother thinks so, Madame Queline thinks so, everybody . . . and you . . . you go and have a fight with one of them!"

"But I couldn't let that skunk get away with talking the way he did about Father!"

"No, of course not, and you were right about that, but, believe me, it's best you don't tell her anything."

Michel shrugged his shoulders. "All right," he said, more calmly, "if you really think so. . . . Now, what about those plates?"

"I'll get them, you might break something. Here, give Fanfan the rest of the tea."

Norette left, walking with her firm little steps. Michel went over to his brother.

"Well, old man, is it true that you're sick? You don't look sick to me! Do you have a temperature?"

"I don't know," he answered, the attention from big brother making him feel important, "but I have a cough." He tried to cough but didn't succeed. He then got his stuffed bear out from underneath the sheets—a tiny bear, threadbare, covered with stains, and with only one eye and three paws left.

"Nono, he is the one who has a cold. He coughs. He caught the raid!"

"The air raid is not a sickness," Michel laughed. "Come, finish your tea." Michel lifted the cup jerkily, spilling all of the tea on the sheet. Fanfan looked at him from the corner of his eye and both of them burst out laughing.

"Darn it!" whispered Michel. "We're going to get it from Norette! Wait, I'll fix it."

And he hid the wet sheet under the blanket. In doing so his hand brushed against Fanfan's little, hot, moist one. "The poor kid really has a temperature," he told himself. "Poor Fanfan!" His bad humor left him, and in a rush of tenderness he stroked his little brother's forehead. Fanfan at once took advantage of his brother's mellow mood. "Tell me a story," he begged. "Just a very, very short one!"

"All right. Which?—the one about the three bears?"

"No, not the three bears! Tell me the one about the chocolate éclair, like on Sunday! Begin. Hurry up!"

Michel sat down on the edge of the bed.

"The chocolate éclair," he began, ". . . they had them at the bakery, you know—the store where we buy bread. At that time, long ago, they also sold there all kinds of pastries. The pastries were spread out on small trays, one next to the other, and there were so many different kinds that you didn't know which to choose; there were cup-cakes, cream puffs, and others with a crust on top, plum tarts, and cherry and strawberry pies. But the most beautiful pastry of all was the chocolate éclair."

"Yes, yes, and what kind was it? How did it taste? Tell me, Michel."

"It was yummy, my Fanfan, and it melted in your mouth, the cream oozing all over. You took a bite and the cream dripped down on your clothes, and you gathered it up with your finger, and you licked your finger so as not to waste a single drop! The cream, you understand, was *inside* the éclair. On top there was chocolate—chocolate icing—hard, and all around the icing was delicious dough, like cake. The dough tasted something like a *brioche.*"

"What is a brioche?"

"I guess you've never tasted that either! A brioche is made out of two balls of dough, a small one on top of a large one. We used to call them 'fat guys,' and they tasted . . . well, they tasted like brioches. How can I describe taste to you?"

"Yes, I see, but, tell me more about the chocolate éclair. Could you eat as many as you wanted?"

"Not really, because they were expensive. But once—it was a Sunday—I remember Daddy buying me three of them after a movie. I ate them right up, one after another. My, was that delicious!"

"Yes," said Fanfan, musingly. "Do you think that Daddy will buy *me* three . . . when he comes back from prison?"

"I'm sure he will . . . three . . . four . . . six . . . eight! We'll eat and eat, and we'll fill our mouths with them, and we'll be all smeared . . . like clowns! Hey! can you imagine how yummy that'll be? And then . . ."

"Come have your lunch, Michel," Madame Sellier called from the next room. Michel hopped, skipped, and jumped cheerfully to the dining room.

"Gee, that story made me hungry! Hurray for lunch!" Michel experienced a wave of joy. He felt an urge to make everyone happy. "I'm going to cheer up Mother," he decided. "I really wasn't nice to her before." But his mother no longer needed comforting, for she had regained her usual serenity. Her face was now calm and she was smiling, and Michel was going to put himself out for nothing. He made up for it by devouring a plateful of Jerusalem artichokes as he listened to Norette describe the morning's events: The suburbs of Paris were bombed the night before, and the baker's wife's cousin lived near there, and she was worried about her safety. Solange had received news from her brother; he told her, by messenger, that he was coming home on Christmas Eve. Soso was so excited that she made three mistakes in her French composition.

"How about you, Norette?" asked Madame Sellier. "Did you do well?"

"Oh yes, it wasn't hard—only one dictation and some questions."

"Don't be so sure," Michel said. "Anyone can make

mistakes. For instance, how do you spell 'pirate'—with one 't' or two?"

"With only one, naturally."

"You are wrong. Two is right."

"Ignoramus!" said Madame Sellier, teasingly. "Your sister is right—'pirate' is spelled with only one 't.'"

Michel put down his fork. "Only one? Then Ménard had some nerve telling me it had two 't's,' and he even wanted me to change it."

"Change what?—your dictation?" asked his mother.

"No, it was . . . oh, nothing! But what nerve he had, just the same! And . . . and . . . Mother, you should have heard Monsieur Touron talk to me *man to man!*"

"What did he say?"

Michel hesitated and chose from among his teacher's remarks only the ones that flattered him most.

"He told me that he understood me."

"Is that so? . . ." remarked Madame Sellier with amusement. "I must say he's luckier than I, because I *don't* understand you . . . and, speaking of understanding you, what possessed you to put your printing set among the noodles?"

"The . . . noodles?" said Michel with disbelief, turning crimson. "Oh, yes . . . that was just for laughs."

His mother sighed. "Some joke! Try to be more sensible, son. I've seen that box hidden all over the apartment. And as for those zeros," she added almost mildly, "I won't punish you this time, but do pay more attention to your schoolwork from now on."

"Yes, Mother, I promise, I promise, I promise!" cried Michel, greatly relieved, and he threw himself into her arms and kissed her very hard. She freed herself gently.

"You'll strangle me, dear! Now, be a good boy and go change your sweater. And you, Norettte, you'll have to do the dishes, my girl. I have a rush job to deliver before two o'clock. I must leave right away."

"Who's going to stay with Fanfan? Would you like me to stay home from school this afternoon?" asked Norette hopefully.

"No, thank you, dear. The Minet sisters are coming over. They offered to take care of Fanfan for me. It's already one twenty-five. . . . I must go."

The two spinsters arrived while Michel was changing his sweater. Both of them were small and both wore trim, old-fashioned, black dresses. They were twins and resembled each other amazingly, and one was never seen without the other.

Mademoiselle Alice brought a lemon and Mademoiselle Marie a picture book. "A whole lemon in times like these!" Madame Sellier exclaimed. "You must keep it for yourselves."

"It will perk him up, the little angel," said Mademoiselle Alice in her fluty voice. And Mademoiselle Marie added, in exactly the same kind of voice, "The picture book is from the concierge. It's an old book of her son's."

"How kind she is!" said Madame Sellier, touched by Madame Queline's generosity. "Now, come, come and say hello to Fanfan."

Michel slipped out, to escape the amenities. He went upstairs to get George and return to school with him. He was still full of the morning's events and felt that he would just about burst if he didn't tell someone about them. As soon as they were out on the street, Michel began to talk fast, swallowing half his words.

"That lousy Gourre!" George said when Michel had finished. "I wish I had been there to help you give him that licking. But, you know, your sister is right! Be careful! Don't forget that those awful people live right in our building."

"So?"

"So, with all those Germans coming and going there, how can you tell what may happen? They may find out about us, my parents and me, get us arrested . . ."

Michel opened his eyes wide. "You? Why?"

"Because I am Jewish," George said with bitterness. "Because it seems it is a crime nowadays to be Jewish.

"But," George continued, "don't I have arms and legs like everyone else? Don't I attend school, like you? Don't I study hard?"

"Sure, and you even got first prize for excellence!"

"Oh, who cares about prizes! And do you know what they'll do to us if they arrest us? They'll send us to Drancy and then to Germany, like they did my uncle Eugene. Mother says awful things happen . . . horrible ones . . . over there. She says that they put you in camps and make you die. . . . Don't think that I'm afraid . . . but I'd hate to die."

"Die?" Michel echoed his friend, the breath catching in his throat. He had once seen a corpse. It was his grandfather. The old man lay on a bed, covered with only a sheet, although it was a very cold day. His head was wrapped in a large kerchief. His eyes were closed. And Michel now suddenly imagined George, his friend George, lying on the same bed, his head swathed in the same kind of cloth. He felt a sickening void and was slightly nauseated.

"And do you believe all that?" he asked, his voice shaking. "You must be kidding."

Then Michel steadied himself and said, making an effort to laugh, "Listen, if that ever happens and they try to arrest you, do you know what I'll do? I'll hide you in my closet, behind my toys, and . . . wait a minute . . . and, yes, afterward you'll put on some of my clothes and you'll say that you are me! All we'll need to do then is take turns being *me*. We'll never be seen together, for instance. . . . Get it? Wouldn't that be funny!"

"Yes, very funny," George said, his voice heavy with sadness.

Michel hooked his arm in George's, and tried desperately to think of something to say that would cheer him up.

"Would you like me to give you my pocketknife?" he asked suddenly. "You know, the red one which you like so much?"

George's eyes beamed. "You mean it? You'd really give it to me? Gee, you are swell!"

Michel, himself feeling happier now, rummaged in his pocket for the knife. He felt it with his fingers, and he also felt the leaflets.

"The leaflets!" he cried. "I forgot all about them. I kept some for you to distribute. Yes, and you must find an assumed name; we each have one now."

"Hurray! I'll choose one too! Let's see, I'll be *Leonidas*. And you—what's your name now?"

"*Hercules*. However, it's hardly worth the trouble *now*, now that the league doesn't exist any more."

"What? What do you mean, it doesn't exist any more?" George asked, looking hard at his friend.

"You know, since Monsieur Touron said that . . ." Michel tried to explain weakly, "since he talked to me man to man about it."

"All he told you was to pay attention in class—just that, and nothing more! If you wanted to, you could do both things. And what about me?—think of me spending a whole morning writing out the next leaflet! No, forget it! You aren't going to drop out. That would really be disgusting of you!"

Michel hung his head in quandary and despair. To whom should he listen—to Monsieur Touron or George? Then he remembered that his teacher was not an unfortunate, that he wasn't Jewish, and he chose to go along with his friend. "All right, I'll stay in the league," he said. "I won't quit the Pirates."

"Good!" George said cheerfully. "I knew you weren't a quitter! The Pirates must continue their daring deeds! But, listen, that affair with Stéphane worries me. We better not talk any more about the league around school. From now on let's all meet in the Luxembourg Gardens—that will be a lot safer." Then he added, "Boy! When I think that you were going to drop out! Wouldn't that have been stupid, old man!" And George kiddingly poked Michel in his ribs with his fist. The two friends grinned at each other and continued on their way to school, arms hooked.

Christmas Eve

Fanfan soon recovered from his illness. The following day his temperature was normal, and he asked to be allowed to get out of bed. Norette was dressing him when the concierge arrived, overjoyed. She brought a letter from Monsieur Sellier, from the prison camp in Germany. He wrote that he was still at the same camp, that he had received their parcel and post card, was well. No, he didn't suffer from the cold. He hoped the war would be over before summer. This news of him was vague and seemed quite distant, for his letter was dated two months before. But at least it was in his own handwriting, and Madame Sellier was heartened. She decided to celebrate Christmas after all. She had just received a large rabbit, some lard, and two cheeses from her mother, who lived in the country. They would invite Solange and her brother, if he came home. They would also invite George and the Minet sisters.

Madame Moscot promised to bake a cake for the occasion. She had somehow invented a cake recipe that didn't require butter and eggs. She and her husband would come down for dessert and coffee. Yes, it was going to be a real Christmas Eve party, such as they hadn't had since the war began.

The children, for their part, prepared a big surprise. Christmas is never real without a Christmas tree, so they bought one with their combined savings. They didn't of course buy it for themselves—oh, no, they were "too old" to care for anything like that. It was for Fanfan, who had never yet seen a Christmas tree except in pictures, and they thought it was high time to do something about that. The children emptied their change purses. Alas, Norette had only three francs and sixty *centimes,* Michel, eighteen *sous* (halfpennies) and a Métro ticket, and Solange, who had been living on a very small allowance from her brother, couldn't spare more than five francs. George was rich, however, and he pulled out of his wallet—yes, he even had a wallet!—a one-hundred franc-bill.

"One hundred francs!" gasped Michel; Norette and Solange gazed at the bill with awe.

"That makes 109 francs 50 centimes," said George after making a rapid calculation. "My friends, we can buy a lot with that! An enormous tree, to begin with."

But they didn't even have "enormous" trees for sale that year, and small ones were so expensive that the children settled for a tiny fir tree, which a florist on Rue Buce sold them at a reduced price because one of its branches was broken. With the twenty francs they had left, Norette bought eight candles. She cut out a star from a piece of silver paper, which she had been saving for a long time with some other treasures. As for paper garlands, it was the Minet ladies who provided those. Michel had let them in on the secret, and they remembered that they had stored away several old garlands at the bottom of a bureau drawer. They also managed to find a small puppet, a red ball, and, wonder of wonders!—a gilded flower.

The children were delighted. How beautiful their tree was going to be! How it would glitter! In the meantime, they hid it underneath the cupboard, where Michel had concealed his printing set, which, forgotten for the moment, now remained on the chest of drawers. They hid the garlands behind the noodles, and Norette put the gilded flower under her pillow "to look at it at night."

Whenever Madame Sellier came near the children, they'd fall silent; she would walk past them with a smile, pretending not to know a thing, although she had long since discovered all the hidden objects when cleaning house. She herself had plenty to do, and on the morning of the twenty-fourth she rose earlier than usual. She had to find some onions with which to brown the rabbit. She had to find some flour, potatoes, and leek for the soup. She got up at dawn in order to get some of the sewing done, so that she'd be free the rest of the day for her other chores. But she hardly felt tired—it was Christmas, in spite of everything. . . . It was a light in the long night of troubles.

At six in the evening, Norette and Solange set the dining room table.

Alain Couture had not yet arrived.

"I hope he comes! I hope he comes!" Solange kept saying plaintively.

"Of course he'll come," Norette kept assuring her. "This evening is not like any other. I'm sure he'll be able to come. Look, he'll sit on Mother's right—that's the place of honor! But hurry and help me, Solange, or we'll be late with you-know-what. . . ."

They got out the checkered tablecloth and the holiday dishes. Mademoiselle Alice had brought over some holly, which Norette arranged on the table around the plates full of cookies and Madame Moscot's cake. Solange kept running from the dining room to the kitchen, where Madame Sellier was browning the rabbit. The appetizing smell of fried lard spread throughout the apartment.

"My, that smells good!" said Michel, sniffing as he came in, followed by George and Fanfan. "Girls, are you ready? It's time now to decorate the . . ."

He stopped and looked at his little brother.

"What are we going to do with him? He can't stay here while we . . ."

"He can come up to our place," said George, ready with a solution. "I'll take him up to Mother. . . . Come along, Fanfan."

Fanfan protested; he wanted to stay with the others, and he wanted to smell the good smell of the rabbit. However, when Solange kissed him and Norette gave him a cookie, he finally let himself be led away.

When the door was closed behind him, Michel, in high spirits, executed a sprightly dance step, saying "To work! And you don't know everything . . . there's another surprise!"

"What else? What surprise?" Solange and Norette insisted on knowing.

"You'll have to wait. I can't tell you yet because George'll be furious if I tell! Gee, what a surprise!"

"Is it a present?" asked Solange, very curious.

"A present? Sort of . . . though it's made of flesh and bone. It was my idea. Monsieur Jean was so nice about it. . . ."

"What will Monsieur Jean have to do with it?" grumbled Norette.

"What will he . . . ? But I must keep my mouth shut. . . . You'll see, you'll see. . . . And Madame Queline promised to . . ."

"What are you telling them?" asked George, who was back now. "I hope you haven't said a word, at least not about *that!*"

Michel was indignant. "Me? What do you take me for? I know how to keep a secret!"

"I don't think so," Solange said, giggling. "'I mustn't say anything' . . . 'Monsieur Jean' . . . 'Madame Queline' . . ."

"Oh, what a blabbermouth!" groaned George. "Now, how about that tree?"

Everyone got busy. Michel pulled out the tree from its hiding place; Solange and George carried a small, round table over to the fireplace; Norette went to get the garlands and the gilded flower.

"What are we going to put the tree in so that it won't tip?" asked Michel.

"I've thought of something," Norette said. "If we can have the soup tureen . . . Mother!" she called out, "Mother, may we borrow the soup tureen?"

"I need it for the soup," Madame Sellier answered from the kitchen. "What do you need it for? . . . Wait, I'm coming."

Norette darted toward the kitchen.

"Oh, Mommie, dear, darling Mommie, I beg you,

don't go in there yet. You mustn't look! . . ." She gave her mother a big kiss and whispered in her ear, "Oh, please, Mommie, pretend you didn't see anything!"

"All right, all right," Madame Sellier said, smiling happily, "I didn't see a thing, not a thing! Go ahead, take the soup tureen; I'll serve the soup from a casserole, and that'll be that. But be sure not to do anything silly."

Norette ran back and got the soup tureen from the cupboard. Michel stuck the little fir tree in it and crammed paper all around the bottom of its trunk. It held fast. George carefully fastened the broken branch with a thread. Solange strung the garlands among the green branches, and Norette found the best spot for the puppet, the red ball, the pink candles, and the gilded flower. There was much giggling, whispering, and happy scurrying about. But when the tree had been decked out in all the delicate finery, the laughter subsided, there was less chattering, and after Norette, perched on a chair, placed the beautiful silver star on the highest branch, there was a complete hush. The children, enchanted, felt their hearts contract with a strange emotion.

"It's magnificent!" Michel was finally able to say. "I didn't think it would be so beautiful! How about lighting the candles right away, so that we can see the full effect?"

"No," said Norette. "They burn too fast. Let's do it this way: first we'll ask everyone to go to the kitchen with Fanfan, then we'll light the candles, open the door . . . and there! . . . Oh, I wish it were already time! What's happened to the Minets—where are they?"

The little old ladies arrived at that very moment, as if they had heard Norette's question. They looked neater than ever in their old black dresses, which they had trimmed with crocheted lace for the occasion. Mademoiselle Marie was carrying a large platter with a beautiful prune pie.

"We made it with the flour we've been saving for the past two years," explained Mademoiselle Alice. "But the piecrust has no shortening," added her sister, regretfully.

"All right, ladies," said Norette, prodding them gently toward the kitchen. "Go in there, please. Mother is expecting you. I'll get Fanfan," she said to the children. "The rest of you light the candles, the matches are on the mantelpiece."

The two boys and Solange made a dash for the matchbox. "Me! Me! Me!" they yelled. Finally they agreed that each would strike one match, and the little candles were lighted, one after the other, making the garlands and the star on the very top gleam.

"Here we are!" cried Norette, reappearing. "Oh! How pretty! Turn off the lights someone. That's even better. . . . You may all come in from the kitchen now!" she called out.

The kitchen door was opened. Madame Sellier came in followed by the old ladies and Fanfan.

"How will Fanfan act? What will he say?" whispered Solange, squeezing Norette's arm with excitement.

The little boy advanced one step and stopped. His eyes filled with wonder, his mouth fell open, he flushed, and he was speechless in the presence of the miracle.

Michel could no longer restrain himself. "Well, my Fanfan, how do you like it?"

Fanfan raised his little finger, pointed at the tree and shrilled in a trembling voice:

"The star, I want the star!"

The spell was broken, everyone burst out laughing; but Fanfan didn't laugh, he remained serious, repeating pleadingly, "I want the star, Mommie!"

"You'll get it soon," Norette promised, giving him a big kiss. "We'll let you have it later, and the puppet and the ball, too. Now it would spoil the lovely tree. . . . You understand, don't you?"

"Are we ever going to eat?" cried Michel.

Then George turned on the lights, and everyone sat down at the table.

Mademoiselle Alice sat near Norette, George next to Fanfan. One place remained empty, at the very end of the table. Solange's eyes filled with tears, and Madame Sellier turned to her, casserole in hand.

"He'll come, my dear," she said to her. "I'm going to keep his soup warm on the stove."

Solange didn't say anything. She forced herself to eat, but her throat was so tight that she couldn't swallow. She didn't dare speak for fear of making the others unhappy, but she was worried. What if something had happened, what if Alain . . . and she kept listening for the sound of footsteps on the stairs.

They were finishing the rabbit when she started, trembling, "Listen!" she said. "Madame Sellier, listen—it's Alain!" She jumped up, upsetting her chair, and ran out onto the landing.

They heard her cry: "Alain!" and almost at once she reappeared, pulling by the hand a tall, thin youth wearing a worn raincoat. His young face looked aged with exhaustion. His hair, a vivid blond, contrasted oddly with the pallor of his face.

"Why, you've become blond!" cried Madame Sellier, astounded.

"Yes," said the young man, removing his coat, "only the hairdresser overdid it a bit. It's too noticeable, don't you think so?"

"How strange—you now resemble Monsieur Jean," remarked Mademoiselle Alice, "you know, Monsieur Jean —the first-floor tenant, across from us."

"Oh, him," Alain scoffed. "The 'trembler'—the one who always moans and groans, that's the one you mean, isn't it? A flattering resemblance, I must say!"

"You should care! You are much handsomer than he," George blurted out.

Madame Sellier laughed. "Much handsomer, indeed," she said. "Now, Alain, please come to the table. You must be starved. I'm going to get your soup. And you, Soso, are you happy now? You aren't going to cry any more, are you?"

"Oh, no, Ma . . . dame . . . Sellier," Solange answered, barely managing not to shed tears of joy. She smiled up at her brother, her eyes moist, and said, "I . . . I didn't think you'd come, I thought . . ."

"You thought what?" he said, shaking her playfully. "Little goose, what did you think would happen to me? You ought to know that I'm made of iron. I've been through everything . . ." and, turning to the grownups, he added, "and, believe me, I've witnessed a pretty thing or two! . . . Oh, look at the lovely little fir tree!"

"It has a star," Fanfan said solemnly.

"*We* bought it," boasted Michel. "But tell us, Monsieur Alain, tell us what pretty things you've seen."

"I didn't really mean 'pretty,'—it's just a manner of

speaking—of course I meant the opposite. For what I witnessed was anything but pretty. But first let me eat my soup. It's very good, Madame Sellier."

Then Alain cut himself a piece of rabbit.

"Well," he finally began, "we had quite a scare, a bad one! I was staying at a farm . . ."

"Where?" asked Michel.

"We don't answer such questions, not nowadays," Alain answered. He continued his story: "I was carrying out a mission, not far from this farm, when I fell into the hands of the Fritzes. The place was swarming with Gestapo men, no less; they are their secret service men. I tried to get away, but nothing doing. I was caught—trapped like a rat!"

"They . . . trapped you?" stammered Solange, and her eyes widened with terror.

Alain squeezed her little hand in his large one.

"Now, Soso, you're not going to cry again, since all that happened in the past, and I'm here now. They no longer have me in their clutches, the *verdouillards*—the green scum in their green uniforms! So, they grabbed me—four or five of them—shoved me into their damn gray car, and off we went to the village. It was crammed with Nazis—from the church to the chicken coops. An officer interrogated me in the school auditorium. And me . . . I played the idiot. . . . I showed them my papers which, naturally, were false ones. But this time they weren't fooled! They took me to the rear, under escort, and led me into a nearby wood, as you might well expect."

"Why the woods?" asked Norette.

"Can't you guess, you foxy one? . . . Well, I knew what was coming. It was no use kidding myself. And, believe me, I wasn't the least bit proud for having allowed myself to be caught like a fool, right in the territory of our own people, the maquisards. The Fritzes were in such a hurry to finish me off that they didn't even take the time to tie my hands. They halted, stood me against a tree, retreated a few steps, took aim . . . 'You're done for,' I said to myself, 'Bon voyage—have a nice trip—Alain Couture!' Then, all of a sudden, there was a tremendous fusillade of shooting. I tell you, my friends, I never heard anything like it. The shots came from all sides—from the thickets, the road. They came fast and furious! Absolutely incredible! Rifles at the ready, the Germans spun around, each cursing worse than the other, and slunk off—the whole bunch of them—toward the edge of the wood. You can imagine that I lost no time waiting for them to return. I spun around that tree and ran for dear life, like one possessed, straight ahead, in the opposite direction. Across one field, another, over one fence, then another, on and on. I finally stumbled into a farmyard. There was still some shooting behind me. You understand, of course, that it was an attack by our men, the *maquis*. And it couldn't have happened at a luckier moment for me! . . . To continue: in the far end of the farmyard a shriveled little man was busy spreading manure. I cried out, 'Hide me!' He stared at me. I must have looked a sight—clothes torn, my face a bloody mess from their blows. Without opening his mouth, the old man pointed to his barn and the ladder leaning against it. I climbed up the ladder into the loft and threw myself on the hay. I must confess I was shaking from head to foot. I didn't know what to expect next. What was he going to do, the silent old man? Was I right in trusting him? In the distance the shooting was subsiding. It was maddening not to know what was happening out there.

"At the end of about half an hour I heard my oldster climbing the ladder. He brought me two eggs and a piece of bread, placed them near me—still without saying a word—went down, and removed the ladder. I grew suspicious and wanted badly to get away. But where? . . . So I ate my eggs and bread and waited. Then I must have slept awhile. I was exhausted—hadn't closed my eyes for three nights. Suddenly I was wakened by the sound of boots in the yard, and I heard the old man say, 'Yes, he's here.' 'That's it!' I thought. 'He has informed on me! I am a goner this time for sure!' And I didn't even try to hide. It was no use. They were already placing the ladder. Heads soon appeared at the opening to the loft . . . and there they were—my comrades!"

Alain stopped talking now, and he slowly passed his hand through his blond thatch. The children gazed at him in wide-eyed wonder, as though they were in the presence of a supernatural creature. The Minet sisters wrung their thin little hands with identical gestures, and Madame Sellier, grown very pale, stared down at her plate. Solange got up and ran to her, sobbing. Madame Sellier took her on her lap.

"You shouldn't have told about such things in front of her," she said softly to Alain. "She's so nervous! But, it's done now. There, there, my darling, calm down. It's an old story now, and your brother is here, safe and sound as you can see for yourself. Come, Soso!"

"And the Germans, what about them?" cried Michel. "They took a powder, right?"

"You bet!" answered Alain. "The maquis' attack was successful, of course. But I left before it was over."

"You did change your identity papers after that, I hope?" asked Madame Sellier.

"Naturally. And that affair explains my visit to the hairdresser. It's too bad, though, that he made my hair look as yellow as brass. . . . It's also too bad that I must leave tomorrow. But it's been great to be home!"

Solange raised her drawn little face. "Tomorrow, already? Oh, no!"

"Now, Soso, don't fret. This time I'm not going far."

"But you look so tired," remarked Mademoiselle Alice with a deep sigh. "Poor youngsters, what a life! What an awful life! When are we going to wake from this nightmare?"

"I'll tell you when. . . ." Alain said cheerfully. "It'll be much sooner than you think! Just wait till the year 1944! But, for the moment, I am here, with all of you, I'm having a good dinner and . . ."

"My goodness!" cried Madame Sellier interrupting him. "Here I am, forgetting to serve the rest of the dinner! Children, you serve the salad, and I'll get the pie."

George and Michel, after exchanging meaningful glances, pushed back their chairs. "We're going to get . . . something," Michel said. And as he passed Norette, he added:

"Now comes the surprise!"

"What are they up to now?" asked Madame Sellier when the boys left the room. "More secrets! Solange, go back to your seat, dear. I'm going to serve the dessert. Norette, please change the plates."

She was cutting the prune pie, everyone watching her

do it, when the door opened and an unexpected visitor entered. It was none other than Father Christmas—long white beard and all, and draped in a large red cloth. George and Michel were hiding behind his back, exploding with suppressed merriment.

"Hello, my friends," said Father Christmas in a deep, deep voice. "Does little Fanfan live here?"

Fanfan, thus singled out, stopped eating his pie and opened his mouth so wide that the prune juice trickled down his chin.

"Y . . . es, monsieur," he lisped.

"Very well," continued Father Christmas. "Has he been a good boy? Is his mother satisfied with him? I've brought him a treat." And he put a candy stick on the table.

"It's Monsieur Jean," cried Norette. "I recognized his voice!"

"Monsieur Jean?" said Madame Sellier. "Monsieur Jean? . . ." And she turned to Alain, her face showing consternation. The young man answered her glance. He frowned and bit his lip.

"Now," said Father Christmas in a natural voice, "I think I can remove my disguise, and it's none too soon. I'm stifling!"

He threw his costume on a chair and adjusted his clothes with precise gestures. As usual, he was very much aware of his appearance. Fanfan looked at him very crossly:

"That wasn't nice," he pouted. "That wasn't nice, Father Christmas! I don't want your candy. I want the star!"

"You may have it now," said Norette. "Here it is, here it is, my little Fanfan."

She took down the star and offered it to her brother. Fanfan grabbed it with both hands and pressed it to his chest; then, hesitating a moment, he reached for the candy and crammed all of it into his mouth, chuckling with delight.

"Gosh, you spoiled it all!" Michel complained, snapping his fingers. "I didn't think you'd guess so soon. But the costume was great, wasn't it, Monsieur Jean? The jacket was made from Madame Queline's curtain—the red one that hangs in her apartment. Did you recognize it, Norette? The beard we made from cotton wool," and, for some obscure reason, Michel roared with laughter at that, adding, "although George nearly ruined it."

"Michel, come to the kitchen, I want to talk to you," his mother said.

She closed the door behind them.

"What's wrong?" Michel asked in a what-have-I-done-now tone.

"Be quiet and listen! Don't you realize what you've done? You shouldn't have let Monsieur Jean come up when Alain was here!"

"Why not?"

"Because Alain came here secretly, because they're looking for him—you know that! Didn't you hear what he just told us? Do you want him to be really shot?"

Michel looked at her dumbfounded, and she added quickly:

"I'm not saying that Monsieur Jean is a traitor, but he's so afraid of everything. Alain came to us because he knew that here he'd find only trustworthy friends, but Monsieur Jean . . ."

"Oh!" Michel exclaimed. "He is all right, Mother, I'm sure of it. He agreed to be Father Christmas!"

"What does Father Christmas have to do with it! It's a matter of life and death. You must understand that! Why didn't you tell me that you were planning that surprise? I'd have stopped it. But it's too late now! At least, do be very careful. Remember, not a word about the Résistance! Warn George and Norette. Solange, I know, won't say anything about it. For heaven's sake, Michel, be careful!"

"Yes, Mother," he promised, although he still didn't quite understand what worried her so.

They returned to the dining room. Monsieur Jean had sat down near Alain.

"I say," he remarked, "*you*'re the one who gave us the real surprise, Monsieur Couture. I didn't expect to find you here."

"You know," Alain answered him coldly, "business . . ."

"That's right, you are in cosmetics aren't you? . . . Not a very good business these days, I'd imagine. It's not like at the drugstore—medicines are very much in demand, whereas perfumes . . . With whom are you employed now?"

Alain hesitated a moment. Mademoiselle Alice stirred uneasily.

"Monsieur Jean, he was about to explain this to us when you arrived. He has been away on a selling trip. As he says, he doesn't lack customers but there isn't enough merchandise; there's even a shortage of perfume bottles, would you believe it!"

"And soap," added Mademoiselle Marie. "He told us that soap . . ."

"But . . ." exclaimed George, "Monsieur Alain didn't . . ."

Michel pulled him by the sleeve and whispered something in his ear. George didn't finish what he was going to say.

"George, it's time for you to go and call your parents," said Madame Sellier. "I'm ready to serve the coffee."

George obeyed. As he opened the door to go upstairs, he bumped into the concierge, who shoved him aside and hurried, out of breath, into the dining room.

"The Germans," she said. "They're here, at the Coutures'."

Madame Sellier covered her mouth with her hand to stifle a cry. Solange threw herself on her brother.

"It's you they're looking for!" she cried, clinging to him. "They are going to take you away! I don't want them to! Oh, help somebody!"

"Be quiet, for God's sake!" Alain said to her roughly, freeing himself. "Madame Queline, did you say they were in our apartment?"

"Yes."

"Then I can still get away."

"Not a chance. One of them is stationed outside and their car is parked in front of the house. I tried to tell the two who came in that there was no one in your apartment, but they didn't listen to me. So I thought it best to let them search it, to give me time to warn you. I opened your door for them with my key—it fits in your lock. What are you going to do, Monsieur Alain? They are sure to come here when they've finished over there."

"Hell!" Alain muttered. "I hardly know! If I could only lay my hands on the rat who informed on me! . . . But

I'm sure I was not followed. . . . Now, let's see . . . there's the window. . . . No, that won't do . . . a three-story jump . . ."

Madame Sellier took him by the arm. She had regained her composure. She pointed to the red coat that still lay on the chair. "Put it on," she said to Alain with authority, "and let me handle things. The boys will help. Madame Queline, I think it's better that you go down. The Germans mustn't find you here. And you, children, stay around the Christmas tree and pretend to be decorating it. The rest of us will remain at the table. Monsieur Jean, take Alain's place. I'll serve the coffee."

The concierge left. Madame Sellier looked around once more to make sure that everything was in order and began to pour the coffee into the glasses, her hand trembling slightly. Alain put on the white beard; George and Michel were kneeling at his chair, fastening the jacket with safety pins.

"Crouch down a little, Alain," Madame Sellier advised. "Try to look shorter. I'll say you are my brother-in-law. What name do you use?"

"Pierre Sénéchal."

"All right, we mustn't . . ."

There was a knock at the door. A harsh voice ordered: "Open up!"

"You go to the door," Madame Sellier said to Norette.

She continued to pour the coffee. Two Germans entered, two uniformed Germans. One of them was fat and purple faced, the other was thin and wore glasses. They stopped on the threshold.

"Oh, my God!" Madame Sellier cried, setting down the coffeepot and looking aghast. "Oh, my God! What is it?"

"Alain Couture," said the fat one, pronouncing the name slowly. "Do you know Alain Couture?"

"Why yes, of course, gentlemen. He's the young man who lives across from us. Are you looking for him? My God, what has he done? Have you rung his bell, yes?"

She pretended to be agitated, in a panic. The thin German approached her. "Your papers!" he snarled.

"Yes, yes, gentlemen, right away. . . . Now where did I put my purse? I hardly know where I am with all this going on! . . . You see, we were having a little Christmas cheer; my brother-in-law disguised himself to amuse the children. . . . Oh, here is my purse. . . . Here, gentlemen!"

She handed her identity card to the thin German, who examined it carefully.

"All right," he said, giving it back to her. "What about the others?"

The Minet sisters reached for their papers, uttering little cries of fright.

"You too, Pierre," said Madame Sellier turning to Alain. "Show them your card! What a thing for 'Father Christmas' to have to do! These are strange times! . . . I won't sleep a wink tonight, that's certain."

Alain, shrinking himself as much as he could, lifted a corner of the red curtain he was wearing and took his wallet out of his pocket. The fat German went over to the lighted Christmas tree as he waited for Alain to get out his papers. Perhaps it brought back some memories, for his glance lingered on it for an instant. But the moment of sentiment passed.

"Now then, let's have that card!" he snapped, looked at it, and said, "All right."

"And here is mine," said Monsieur Jean.

The fat German took his card, but didn't hand it back right away. The two Germans exchanged some rapid comments, in low tones. They were saying *"Tall . . . Blond."* The thin German raised his revolver.

"Come with us!" he said, aiming the gun at Monsieur Jean.

Monsieur Jean turned ashen pale and withdrew a step. "Me?" he stammered. "Why me? For heaven's sake! I didn't do anything. I . . ."

He looked around the room, baffled, and his eyes went from Alain to Madame Sellier. The look that Alain returned was cold and hard, that of Madame Sellier, beseeching. Monsieur Jean braced himself, trying to conquer his fear, and approached the Germans.

"It's a mistake," he said, "an awful mistake, but I guess there is no other way out but to go along with you. Let's be on our way, then!"

He left with the two uniformed men, nervously adjusting his tie. No one moved in the room. They listened to the sound of the heavy footfalls becoming fainter from floor to floor. Then they could hear a car start down in the street. Solange threw herself into her brother's arms so violently that the white beard came off.

"They didn't arrest you," she wailed. "Oh! I was so afraid! Alain! Alain! Alain!"

She gagged, unable to catch her breath because of a nervous spasm. They had to bring her to. They put a cold cloth on her forehead. But she continued to tremble all over and to cling to her brother, as though she were trying to make sure that he was still there. Norette kept kissing her, the Minet women caressed her, and George and Michel were casting hostile glances at Alain.

"Monsieur Jean didn't do anything! Not a thing!" Michel finally said with angry conviction.

"No, he didn't," said Alain rather sharply, "but they mistook him for me—that's what happened. I understood perfectly what the Germans whispered to each other: 'Tall . . . Blond . . .' That miserable hairdresser is the cause of all this trouble, and that streaky hair coloring he gave me. . . . Poor devil, that Monsieur Jean! It's tough letting someone else be taken in your place, but what could I do? I had to!"

"But he didn't do anything," repeated George. "It was you, not him!"

Alain didn't answer. Madame Sellier motioned to the two boys to come to her. "I know exactly what you are thinking," she said to them, "but you are old enough to understand one thing: Alain's life doesn't belong to him now; it belongs to his underground group, not to him."

"But Monsieur Jean didn't do anything!" Michel repeated for the third time.

"You are right, Michel. But since he is innocent, he has a chance to get out of it. They may verify his identity papers; they may release him. But Alain—he'd be done for. And how can one know what a prisoner will or will not tell when they torture him?"

She was silent for a moment, then added, stressing each word, "Alain couldn't act otherwise. It was his duty to keep quiet."

The two boys nodded their heads, indicating that they had understood.

"I'm leaving," said Alain, rising. "I've caused you enough trouble. And as far as all of you are concerned, my advice is that you be on your guard. To be quite blunt about it, I'm not too sure of Monsieur Jean—he might talk, to save his skin, and tell them everything."

"I don't think so," Madame Sellier said thoughtfully. "If he were going to talk, he'd have done so at once, but you saw how he had himself under control. Besides, he looked at me before leaving, and there are glances that you can't misunderstand. No, I don't think he'll betray you. But, if you leave now, where will you go?"

Alain shrugged his shoulders with resignation.

"Don't worry about me, I'll hole up somewhere. I'm used to this. That's my life these days. I seldom sleep in the same bed two nights in a row . . . that is, when I *have* a bed. . . . Listen!" he suddenly said, jumping up. "Isn't someone knocking?"

"Three little taps," said Norette. "It's the concierge."

It was indeed Madame Queline. She came up to learn how the affair with the Germans had ended. When she heard that Alain was about to leave, she raised her arms in a gesture of fear.

"Don't take any chances," she warned him. "They've left someone to watch the house. You can see him from up here—through that window."

Alain walked over to the window and peered down, cautiously, so as not to be seen from below. Yes, there was a man posted in the shadow of the entrance to the building on the opposite side of the street.

"Damn them!" he said furiously. "They think they got me, but they also hope to snare some others, and they've set a trap. What in the world possessed me to come here this evening!"

He began to pace the room, breathing heavily. Mademoiselle Marie whispered something in her sister's ear. Mademoiselle Alice nodded and smiled.

"Come and stay with us," they said simultaneously.

"With you? Where is that?" asked Alain.

"In our apartment—on the first floor," answered Mademoiselle Alice. "Two old maids like us, who would suspect anything? We have a couch in the parlor. . . . We'll spread a green blanket on it. . . ."

"The mattress is a bit hard," added Mademoiselle Marie apologetically, "but we have a good pillow for you to use."

Alain gave the invitation some thought. "If you'll let me," he then said. "Just for the night, at least. Tomorrow I'll think of something."

The old ladies thanked him. They were somewhat confused—one would have thought that Alain was doing them a favor by agreeing to hide in their place. Beaming with happiness, they soon left with their new boarder, clucking their tongues at how bad he looked and how much he needed sleep.

The concierge caught up with them on the landing. "What about the Gourres?" she said, barely audibly. "Their German officer is visiting them at this very moment. They are guzzling champagne together, and the kids were hanging around the hall just before. They mustn't see Monsieur Alain. Wait here, I'll check." And she leaned over the railing to see. "No," she said a moment later, "I don't see any of them. Go on, but be careful when you pass their floor."

The small group cautiously descended the stairs, while George went to tell his parents what had happened. Madame Sellier remained alone with the children in the deserted dining room, where the Christmas tree was still alight, with its puppet and the gilded flower. Fanfan was asleep at the table, his nose against his precious star. Norette soon put him to bed.

"Norette," her mother said when she returned, "Solange will stay with us tonight. She'll sleep with you. You'll be a bit cramped, but you'll manage."

"Good!" cried Norette, clapping her hands. "Did you hear that, Soso, did you hear? We're going to play lots of games, aren't we?" she whispered. "It'll be great fun!"

"Yes . . ." Solange said absently. "Do you think Alain will sleep well at the Minets? Tell me, Madame Sellier, do you think he'll like it there?"

"Like it?" said Madame Sellier. "Why, my dear, they'll coddle him like a baby. There'll be a hot-water bottle for him, a featherbed, and lime-blossom tea; and breakfast in bed next morning. One would think you didn't know them. . . ."

"I guess you're right," said Solange, feeling for the moment a little less anxious about her brother. A faint smile lifted the gloom from her face as she took Norette's hand, saying, "Are we really going to play games? Let's go!"

Madame Sellier kissed the two girls good night and watched them and Michel go to the other room. When the children's chattering stopped, she sighed, cleared the table, and began to wash the dishes. The tremendous effort she had had to make to stay calm and keep her wits about her had worn her out. She felt achy all over and could hardly stand up. At least she was alone now and she could give vent to her feelings without worrying about being seen by the children. Slowly and in silence her face was covered with tears; they dropped one by one into the dish bowl, unnoticed by her. "Come now," she kept saying to herself, trying to stop crying, "Alain is safe for the time being and that's what counts. But what about tomorrow?" she worried. "And that poor Monsieur Jean who has so little fight in him . . ." No, it was all too much, too much! she felt. And the tears would not stop flowing.

Later, as she recrossed the dining room after stacking the clean dishes in the cupboard, she stopped in front of the Christmas tree. All the candles had burned down except one, which still flickered under the garlands, its small flame quivering. The flame would shoot up, shrink again, then flare up once more; it seemed that it would die any second. Madame Sellier, her eyes fixed on the faltering flame, rested her cheek against the tree's cool branches. She stood thus, thinking back to Christmas trees in the past and to other things that had comforted her in her childhood; the tree when she was eight years old, the one when she was twelve. Then she recalled the first Christmas tree which she had decorated for Michel and the first one for Norette, and lastly, the one in the year 1938, which her husband had bought at the Market of Flowers, and which they had had to shorten because it had been so tall. "Next year he'll buy one for us again," she said to herself. "Oh, if that would only come to pass!" She continued to stand there, motionless and pensive, until the little flame went out. Then she walked away noiselessly, and, after looking once more at the sleeping tree, went to bed.

Daniel

The next day brought new troubles. During the night Solange had developed a high temperature. She was delirious and kept calling for her brother. Madame Sellier had to take her into her own room, so that Norette could get some sleep. At seven o'clock in the morning she still had a high fever. Very worried, Madame Sellier sent Michel for Doctor Ménard. He came almost at once. When he arrived Solange was no longer delirious, but she was still very agitated. Her face, normally so pale, was flushed, and she complained of a severe headache.

"Nothing wrong with her lungs, nothing in her throat," said the doctor. "It looks like a bad case of nervous upset. Has the child suffered some kind of shock?"

Madame Sellier murmured, "Yes." Without asking for details, the doctor wrote out a prescription and advised maximum rest and calm. Before leaving, he asked Madame Sellier, "Your son, has he been doing well in school? Mine doesn't study at all, absolutely not. I find him hiding in all kinds of corners, doing something with green pieces of paper. . . . I keep wondering what he's up to.

Actually, I understand what ails him; their heads are full of the Résistance—all the kids carry on this way. . . . Speaking of her," he added, turning his head toward the patient, "what do you hear of young Couture?"

"Oh, you know, he travels all the time; he sells cosmetics . . . ," replied Madame Sellier, blushing a little for telling a falsehood.

"Yes, I know . . . but . . . it may some day be useful for you to know that I treat nonpolitical prisoners at Fresnes—I have certain connections there. So, if I can ever be of help to you in that regard, please call on me. Good night now, and don't be alarmed—the child's temperature will no doubt drop as suddenly as it rose."

Madame Sellier shook his hand without comment. "Fortunately, there are good people in this world!" she said to herself, somewhat encouraged. "But what will I do with the patient?" She couldn't even think of sending Solange to her own place. She decided to put her in Norette's room. Michel and George went and got her little cot, which they squeezed, somehow, into the narrow space between the chest of drawers and Norette's bed, and the dozing Solange was transferred onto it.

Norette was delighted. She was going to have her friend all to herself; they weren't going to have to part, day or night.

"Mother, you won't need to take care of her," Norette said. "I'll do it, I'll do everything, everything!"

"Very well," her mother said, "since you are determined to do *everything*, suppose you begin by not talking so loudly. The doctor advised rest, lots of rest. . . . Did you hear that, boys? Did *you* hear, Fanfan? Please play in the other room, all three of you."

"Did the man say that Solange should drink lime-blossom tea?" asked Fanfan, following his mother into the dining room. "Will I drink some, too? Me too?"

"You'll have some if you are good," she said, hugging him, "but now let me sweep up, my darling!"

She tidied the place quickly, then got ready to go to the store for some bread and to the pharmacy for Solange's medicine. On her way down she stopped at the Minets. Alain, washed, combed, but not shaved, was pacing restlessly in the parlor, taking big steps in the tiny room. The two sisters were looking on, distraught.

"He has hardly slept," sighed Mademoiselle Alice, "and this morning he had only a bit of barley coffee; he needs more than that to strengthen him. He'll surely get sick this way!"

"And he couldn't even shave," added Mademoiselle Marie. "Where does one buy a razor?"

"You needn't buy one," said Madame Sellier. "I'll lend him my husband's." And turning to the young man, she asked, "What's going to happen now, Alain? What did you decide to do?"

He stopped pacing and stood in the middle of the room. "I'm trapped," he said, shrugging his shoulders. "That spy is still down there, the same one, or maybe another. The house is under surveillance. My comrades are waiting for me . . . and today is the day for distributing assignments; I was supposed to spend the last two evenings typing out information and instructions. And here I am, cornered. . . . Hell! What could have gone wrong? Who could have informed on me?"

"Are you sure that you weren't followed?" asked Mademoiselle Alice.

"Yes, I'm sure of it! What worries me most is that they came to look for me *under my right name*. No one knows it where I now 'work.' On the other hand, they arrested Monsieur Jean because he was blond. I am *now*, and it was only yesterday afternoon that I had the color of my hair changed, only yesterday afternoon. . . . Someone must have seen me leave the hairdresser's or it was someone who later noticed me coming into this house."

The three women exchanged glances, the same thought occurring to all three of them. "Did you by chance run into one of the Gourres as you were coming into the building?" asked Madame Sellier.

"You mean the owners of the paint store? No, I don't think so. There was an old woman standing on the sidewalk and a boy . . . Ah, wait a minute—now that I think of it, perhaps that was one of their sons. The boy turned around and stared after me as I passed him. Oh, those filthy traitors! If it was they! . . . To think that they are so near, right over my head—that all I'd have to do is go up one flight of stairs and . . . But, I'll take care of them at the proper time! Right now there are more important things to think about."

He dropped into a chair. It creaked. Mademoiselle Marie gave a little start.

"I must warn my comrades," continued Alain, as if talking to himself. "The Germans aren't clever, but once they get on your track, they don't give up—I've had some experience with that. And to tell the truth, I'm not too sure about Monsieur Jean. If he bungles it during the questioning, he may tell them all he knows."

Madame Sellier had to admit that Alain might be right. "There is only one solution," she said. "Someone other than you must keep the appointment with your contacts and tell them what happened."

"That's exactly what I thought! But whom can I send? You realize it must be someone who could leave this house unnoticed, because of that man watching below . . . a child, for instance . . . Maybe we can send your son."

"No you don't!" said Madame Sellier. "Not Michel!" She raised her hands as if to ward off deadly danger.

Alain smiled bitterly. "Have it your way," he shrugged. "But we can't very well send the Moscot boy, can we?"

"George? . . . His parents are scared to death as it is. You can ask them, but I don't think it would be wise. I must leave now," she added abruptly, and, picking up her bag, she fled, as if from an enemy.

She walked up the familiar street, staring straight ahead, too upset to care about where she was going. "They're all the same—those people of the Résistance," she said to herself. "'The group, the group' . . . that's all they know! Alain ought to be ashamed of himself," she went on, almost aloud. "How can he involve himself in things like that when he has a sister to raise? A sister . . . Why, come to think of it, I didn't even tell him that Solange was ill. But what does he care that she's ill and that I am burdened with taking care of her? What does he care about Monsieur Jean's life, or Michel's? Other people's lives are cheap to him!" Madame Sellier knew that she didn't really believe a word of what she was saying about Alain, but it was doing her good to say it. At that moment she detested him.

She bought the bread, giving the baker two ration tickets too many; and she noticed when she arrived at the drugstore that she had unintentionally torn up the prescription. After assembling the pieces, with difficulty, she got the medicine and walked home, still deep in thought.

Fanfan was in the dining room, playing with his teddy bear. "Where's Michel?" she asked him even before setting down her shopping bag.

Michel appeared from the next room, book in hand. "Here I am," he said cheerfully. "What is it? Do you want me to go on an errand?"

His mother drew him to the window and looked at him for a long time. "Have I done something bad?" he asked uneasily.

She didn't answer his question, she merely shook her head, and then said without wavering:

"Put your things on, dear, and go down to see Alain at the old ladies'. Tell him this: 'Mother has changed her mind. She wants me to go, but only this once.' Did you listen carefully to what I just said? Repeat it!"

"Mother has changed her mind. She wants me to go, but only this once."

"Good. Alain will tell you what he wants you to do; it is taking a message to his comrades, since he can't get away. But be very careful when you leave the building—remember the man who is watching this house from across the street. And when you are through with the errand, come home at once. I'll be waiting for you."

Michel's eyes danced with joy. "I understand!" he cried. "I understand! I'm going to work for a group! Oh, Mother! Thanks, thanks! I'm so happy! Can I take George along?"

"No, you mustn't even say anything to him about it. Here, take this . . ." and she pointed to a platter on the cupboard. "Take it with you—it belongs to the old ladies. They forgot it here yesterday. It'll explain your visit to the Minet sisters, in case you run into one of the Gourres on the stairs."

Michel was going to kiss her, but she held him off gently, contenting herself with stroking his head lovingly.

She helped him get dressed, tied his muffler, and said to him softly, "Go now, go on."

Michel was in a state of exaltation. He suddenly felt a contempt for the Pirates of the Résistance. What he was about to do was the real thing, with real men! How he wished right now that he would meet Stéphane and thumb his nose at him, without seeming to, of course. Someone was coming up the stairs. It was not Stéphane; it was his brother Louis. Normally, Michel never talked to this one, but on a day like this . . .

"Did you have a pleasant holiday?" Michel asked him.

"You bet!" Louis replied. "We had turkey!"

"Watch out, old man, turkey from the enemy is poisonous. Aren't you sick to your stomach this morning?"

"Not at all, and I drank champagne, the kind *you* never drank! And what kind of holiday did you have?"

Michel knew what Louis was hinting at—the visit from the Germans—and, his face brightening, he boasted: "Couldn't have been better! We had a Christmas tree—a real one—and we had delicious cake, the kind I bet *you* never ate! The Minet ladies baked it, and I am returning their platter to them now. Good-by!"

"Good-by!" said Louis, and he continued up the stairs, looking a little put out.

"You can't make me jealous, no matter how hard you

try, you dirty collaborator!" muttered Michel. He pressed the bell button hard. Mademoiselle Marie came to the door. Michel greeted her, and without losing any time hurried into the parlor. Alain looked at him with surprise.

"Mother has changed her mind," Michel burst out. "She wants me to go, but only this once! Oh, you're neat, Monsieur Alain! . . . Say, can't I really take George along? That would be so much more fun—if he went with me!"

Alain frowned. "Fun . . . fun . . ." he said sourly. "I don't think you have the right attitude; there's nothing to provide you with fun in all this, and if you're going to be silly about it . . ."

Michel flushed and looked up at him with the innocence of a young boy. "You can depend on me, Monsieur Alain," he said with sudden seriousness. "I'll do the job, and I'll do it right."

"I hope so," said the young man, still rather sourly. "So, here it is: did you ever take the Métro—the subway?"

"Of course! When I deliver Mother's work, I get on at the Vaugirard station."

"Good. You'll take the Métro at Réaumur-Sébastopol and you'll get off at Villiers. Memorize this as you would a history lesson. Got that straight?"

"Yes."

"Then, get off at Villiers, follow the Boulevard des Batignolles in the direction of Clichy, and turn into Rue Boursault—on your left—*Bour-sault.* Follow this street for two blocks . . . no, three . . . then you'll be at the corner of Rue Bridaine . . . *Bri-daine.* Now repeat!"

"Boulevard des Batignolles, Rue Boursault, Rue Bridaine," Michel repeated diligently.

"That'll do. At the corner of Bridaine there is a café—the *Rendez-Vous;* the name is printed on the window. You'll go in and you'll ask to see the owner. He's a fat, dark-complexioned man with a very red nose. His name is Carpot. Repeat!"

"A fat, dark-complexioned man, whose name is Carpot."

"When you find him, make sure that no one can hear you, and tell him very softly: 'Étienne sent me.' Watch yourself, and whatever you do, don't use my right name! The owner will take you to a rear room, and there you'll find a blond young woman—she's rather stout. You'll explain to her what has happened to me—you can leave out the details. Tell her that I'll get away from here as soon as I can, but, in the meantime, they must prepare things for the couriers. You'll also say that someone will be at the appointed place tomorrow, at the agreed hour, and that it'll definitely be me. That's all. Here is money for your Métro tickets. You may go now."

Michel took the money and left, after putting the platter on the table. Alain's cold tone bothered him a little, and he didn't feel quite so enthusiastic. "He could at least have thanked me," he thought. "And how does he expect me to remember all that? It's even more complicated than the rivers of Asia! Villiers . . . Batignolles . . . Bour . . . Bour . . . what was the rest of it? I don't remember any more!" He considered going back and asking Alain, but lacked the nerve and continued on his way, feeling very upset. "Bourd . . . Bourf . . . Bourl! . . ." Everything got mixed up in his brain. By the time he reached the Réaumur subway station he no longer knew whether it was the fat man who was blond or the young woman, and whether he was to say that Étienne sent him or Marcel. But, at the Villiers station the correct name of the street suddenly popped into his head: "Boursault," yes, that was it. "Boursault!" He also remembered at the same moment that having been so absorbed in his mission, he had completely forgotten to watch the spy when leaving the house. Maybe the man was following him . . . no doubt he was! Michel turned around fearfully, but saw no one. "Nonsense," he told himself. "I leave the house many times a day. Why should the spy have bothered about me today?" Turning left, he walked up Rue Boursault, and after crossing several more streets, finally came to Alain's café. *At the Rendez-Vous* was printed on the windowpane. Michel stopped short. He had never before entered a café alone. At least if George were with him! . . . He heaved a big sigh and went inside through a narrow door, pretending to be casual about it.

Two women were drinking lime-blossom tea in the corner of the room, and a fat, swarthy man was behind the counter, rinsing glasses. His nose flamed red between his sallow cheeks. He was no doubt the owner, but what a beak he had, a real clown's nose! Michel, suppressing a wild urge to giggle, approached the man doggedly. He raised himself on his tiptoes to look taller, and whispered:

"You are Monsieur Carpot, yes? Étienne sent me."

The man put down his dish towel. "Why, it's you, sonny," he gushed. "Well, how goes it at home? My wife will be glad to see you! She is in the back—go on in and say hello to her."

He led Michel into a dismal, musty room. A large billiard table filled it almost from wall to wall. At the very end of the room, sitting at a marble-topped table, was a young blond woman, rather plump. She was smoking a cigarette.

"This kid was sent by Étienne," the man said, speaking rapidly. Then he left, closing the door behind him. Michel stood there swinging his arms. The young woman put out her cigarette in a saucer and looked at him with a puzzled expression.

"Well, come closer," she said with impatience. "What did Étienne want you to tell me? Isn't he coming?"

"He can't come," answered Michel. "He is . . . trapped; they almost arrested him."

And he began to describe the search by the Germans. Alain had said that he didn't need to go into many details, but, carried away by his story, he mentioned them anyway, describing the fir tree, the rabbit, Father Christmas.

The young woman interrupted him with exasperation. "That's enough! I don't care about your tree! Now, is that all?"

"Oh, no, madame, Al . . . Étienne said that you'd have to somehow manage to prepare the instructions for the couriers. He'll come here tomorrow, at the same time, if he can get away."

"*Flûte et flûte,*" said the irate blond woman. "That's all I need—with all the work still to be done! I can see I'm in for two more nights without sleep! Anyway, you can tell Étienne that I got his message. Tell him also that tomorrow he won't be seeing me but Daniel. . . . Did you get that?—*Daniel.* And give these papers to Étienne."

"What's in them?" asked Michel.

"You needn't know that. Take them and hide them somewhere inside your clothes!"

Michel took the sheaf of stencils and slipped it under his sweater.

"And try not to get arrested with those on you," added the young woman, rising from her seat. "That's all, you may go now."

Then her face suddenly softened and she said in a gentler tone, "You are certainly a brave kid!"

Michel left promptly. He was about to go out the front door when the owner called him back. "Say, kid, how about a drink?"

Michel retraced his steps, blushing a dark red at the thought of having a drink in a café. The owner selected a bottle from the shelf behind him. "Dubonnet," he said. "Dubonnet—vintage '43 only, of course, but it's not too bad!"

He filled two glasses, emptied his in one gulp, and wiped his mouth with the back of his sleeve. "Now it's your turn—bottoms up!"

"Yes, monsieur!" said Michel, and gulped down his glassful in the same way the owner did. He choked and coughed.

"Ha, ha, ha!" the man laughed. "You aren't used to the stuff, are you, my little man! Well, so long, now. Give my best to your folks, don't forget!"

Michel left. He felt very dizzy, the Dubonnet, vintage '43, having gone to his head; he also felt as happy as when he received an "A" in school. He had memorized his "lesson" well, and Monsieur Alain would congratulate him this time! But what were all these papers about, he wondered. "Who cares!" he told himself. "After all, they don't concern me." Then he thought about the drink he had had with the café owner—"man to man"! This reminded him of his teacher. What would Monsieur Touron have said if he had seen him in the company of that blond girl—after having urged him to study hard and not to get involved in "other things"? Would he understand? Yes, he would, Michel was convinced. He would be pleased with him.

Michel took the Métro. The cars were full of Germans. Their knapsacks were all over, even between the legs of the passengers. The people glared at the Fritzes, enraged and stubbornly silent. Michel couldn't resist whistling. These Germans had no inkling of what important papers he, Michel, had on him—right there, under his sweater. He deliberately pulled down his sweater to relish the sound of the crackling papers. It seemed to him that his neighbors, those of them who were his countrymen, regarded him with friendliness, seemingly guessing what he had just accomplished. He glowed with pride.

Before entering the house, he looked around for the spy and saw him pacing at his post, warming his hands with his breath. "All's well," he thought. No one had followed him. He darted into the entrance and hurried to the Minet apartment, flushed with happiness.

"Well?" Alain asked him.

"Well, I did it! I saw the blond girl, and she said that she understood your message. She will expect you tomorrow, or rather, no, it will not be she, it will be Daniel. And she gave me some papers."

He rummaged in his clothes and got out the stencils. Alain suppressed a swear word.

"Triple idiots!" he growled. "What do they expect me to do with these? I have no typewriter! You don't happen to have a typewriter around here?" he asked of no one in particular.

Mademoiselle Alice emerged from the kitchen, enveloped in a large blue apron. "A typewriter? Good heavens, we don't have one. . . . Here, Michel, please take this razor back to your mother, and thank her for me. Ask her to excuse us for not coming upstairs to thank her personally, but we're about to make some pancakes."

"Pancakes . . . pancakes no less," Michel muttered on his way upstairs. "He's certainly living it up! You'd think everyone owes him everything." A stifled cry interrupted his reflections. It had come from his mother, who was leaning over the railing.

"At last!" she said weakly. "Is . . . is everything all right?"

"Quite," said Michel, his eyes flashing. "And you ought to have seen me having a drink with the owner! He gave me Dubonnet! The real stuff. And was it good! And did it burn my throat!"

The table had been set and the rest of the rabbit stew was simmering on the stove. Michel ran into the room where the girls were. Solange was asleep, buried in her sheets; strands of light hair stuck to her damp forehead; she was holding her doll tightly in her arms. Norette, darning a woolen vest, was sitting on a low stool near the night table, which was full of medicines.

"Soso just fell asleep," she whispered. "You came home very late—where were you?"

"I went for a little walk."

"Is that so? . . . I wouldn't be surprised if it's still that business with the printing set."

"You think so? No, it's something far more important! You know . . . hmm . . . yes, you guessed right. It *is* the printing set."

"Obviously," Norette said with an air of great superiority. "You can't hide anything from *me!*"

Michel couldn't resist a mysterious smile. "That Norette, with her airs, wouldn't she be mad if she knew the truth!" he thought. "Have you seen George?" he asked her. "Has he been here?"

"No, he hasn't. The Moscots refuse to budge from their apartment, and they won't let George go out. I hear they've been very upset since last night. If anyone finds out that they are Jewish . . ."

"What makes you think anyone would find out?" Michel snapped. "What nonsense you talk, you silly! I think I'll go up to see George later."

After lunch Madame Queline came up. She reported that the Gourres had just left and that they had informed her, in passing, that they'd not be back before midnight. The house was rid of them till then.

This caused a general rejoicing. Madame Moscot left her apartment, though still very upset; Madame Sellier spent more than an hour comforting her. She finally calmed down and went up to get a can of fruit, which George took over to the Minet ladies. Monsieur Moscot sent along some cigarettes for Alain; Madame Sellier added some noodles; and the concierge contributed a jar of jam that she had been saving, with other goodies, for her son's return. The Minets came to thank everyone personally, but they could talk of nothing else than finding a typewriter for Alain.

"Monsieur Alain is desperate," they said. "He ate almost nothing for lunch. He didn't even finish his second pancake, he's been so despondent. Where can we get hold of a typewriter? Of course there is Monsieur Jean's. . . ."

"So," Alain said, "all we have to do is borrow it!"

"But his door is locked," said the concierge.

"Locked? Then try your key; it fit our lock yesterday evening!"

Madame Queline tried her key and succeeded in opening the door. When they located the typewriter, another difficulty arose: the carriage didn't work; it was impossible to move it, either to the right or to the left. Alain fretted. Time was passing. It was important to finish everything before the Gourres came home, considering the infernal noise that typewriter would make.

"Why don't we ask old man Lampion to fix it?" suggested Madame Sellier. "He must know a lot about machines—he's always tinkering with something. Besides, he works at a printer's."

The matter was discussed. True, it would mean taking a risk, but old man Lampion was a courageous man and, after all, he, too, hated the Germans. Fortunately, he was right there now, alone in his room, at home because of the Christmas holiday. Madame Sellier volunteered to approach him about the typewriter. After hearing her first few words, the old man interrupted her:

"No need to tell me any more; don't trouble yourself.

I know what's involved, and I assure you that you couldn't have come to a better person. My employer, you know, doesn't limit himself to printing German obscenities. I'd like you to visit a certain house in the suburbs some day . . . but, mum is the word! Now let's have a look at your machine."

He examined the carriage and announced that it would be as good as new within a half hour. Twenty minutes later he brought the typewriter over to the Minet apartment. Alain seized it as if it were a treasure and, for the first time since the previous day, his strained features relaxed. Now he needed some paper. Monsieur Moscot searched his wardrobe shelf and found two almost intact reams of paper under one of his shirts. The sisters installed Alain in a room giving on the courtyard, from which the noise of the typewriter couldn't be heard in the street, and the young man set to work. He typed without a pause until dark, without even taking a break to have his dinner, which Mademoiselle Marie had brought to him on a tray. When the rasping tac-tac-tac of the typewriter finally stopped, toward midnight, the tenants sighed with relief; now the Gourres could return.

Doctor Ménard had called at six that evening. Solange's fever had subsided and she had wakened in a much calmer state. She was no longer delirious, but with her consciousness she had also regained her fears. She asked for news of her brother. When Madame Sellier assured her that he was safe, a wan smile spread over her face, and she closed her eyes with relief. Norette watched over her the entire night and dozed off only toward morning. Coming into her room at eight o'clock, her mother found her fast asleep and didn't have the heart to wake her. She quickly made breakfast for Michel and Fanfan and went down to the Minet's. A man was still standing watch outside, and Alain, as on the previous day, was pacing the room nervously. Madame Sellier did not wait for Alain to suggest it:

"It's all right," she said. "Michel will go back there this morning; give me the papers you've typed."

And Michel was soon once more on his way to the little café. He wasn't thinking about Alain, however—his thoughts were full of George. After having vainly fought the temptation, he confided yesterday's adventure to him. George had envied him, but when Michel, in concluding his story, had scoffed at the Pirates of the Résistance, his friend had said, not mincing words:

"Naturally, I kind of expected this. First it was Monsieur Touron, now it's Monsieur Alain! Who do you think you are, anyway? If that's the way it is, *I* am going to lead the Pirates of the Résistance, and I assure you the league will do good work! Only, remember, when Monsieur Alain leaves, nothing doing—don't think you can come back and ask me to give you back your former position. And you better let me have that printing press. *You* won't need it now."

Michel had given him the box with an air of indifference, but, if the truth were known, he was sorry now that he had relinquished it. What, indeed, would he do when Alain was gone? How long the days would seem!—long and monotonous. He arrived at the café in a thoughtful mood. The blond girl wasn't there. He found in her place a dark-skinned man with a solemn face. He appeared to be as tired as Alain.

"How's Étienne?" the man asked him in an incisive voice.

"He's still over there," answered Michel. "He hasn't been able to leave because of the spy . . . but he typed the instructions." Then Michel drew the papers from inside his shirt in a casual way—yes, he was beginning to get used to this sort of thing.

"So," said the man, "you're catching on fast. You look to me like a boy who has his wits about him! . . . Tell Étienne that he must manage to get away, come what may. I need him and I'll expect him tomorrow, at the Center. After ten."

"Yes, monsieur."

But Michel couldn't help feeling reluctant to leave. The man fascinated him. Such strength emanated from him that his very appearance gave one courage. A surge of heroism filled Michel's being. He suddenly visualized himself standing before Daniel at some future time, in the same spot. He had just accomplished a very daring mission for him, and Daniel was saying: "Well done!" Almost at the same moment the opposite thought struck him—alas! he'd never see Daniel again, he'd never come back there, since Alain was going away. A shudder went through him, and he said in a shaking voice, "Oh, monsieur, couldn't . . . couldn't I work for you some more? Don't you need me?"

Daniel looked at him gravely and nodded his head, smiling faintly. "Why not?" he said.

"Thank you! Thank you! When? Tomorrow?"

"No, not tomorrow, but I might certainly need you soon."

"Really? Then let me give you my address."

"Étienne knows it," Daniel said. "That's all that's necessary."

Michel opened his mouth, wanting to say something else, but what he felt at that moment was so overwhelming that he couldn't find words to express it. He left in a trance. He didn't even hear the café owner calling to him from the bar, "How about another Dubonnet?" The walk to the Métro seemed interminable. When he finally arrived at the Minet apartment, he was completely out of breath. Excited and exhausted, he had some difficulty relaying the message from Daniel.

"I'm going to leave this evening," said Alain after hearing Daniel's message.

"That would be madness!" exclaimed the old ladies. "You'll be arrested! Heavens, aren't you comfortable here?"

"I must leave this evening," Alain repeated curtly.

And he did in fact leave that same evening. He had changed his raincoat for an old overcoat belonging to Monsieur Sellier, and Monsieur Moscot had given him a beret, which he pushed down almost over his ears, in order to hide his conspicuously blond hair. Besides, the street was so dark that no one could tell blond hair from brown. It was snowing. Alain departed as he had come, in the snow, and in the night. While Michel was stationed on the landing to watch the door to the Gourre apartment, Alain had quickly taken leave of the aged sisters and informed Madame Sellier that he would not be back for a long time, the house no longer being safe for him. A large truck had just been parked in front of the adjacent building. Alain took advantage of this, quickly skirting around it. The tenants, their faces glued to the windows, watched his indistinct figure disappear around the corner. There was no sign of the spy.

"I hope he hasn't followed him," said Madame Sellier coming away from the window. "It's strange that he isn't anywhere to be seen, that one."

"Alain should have stayed on," lamented Mademoiselle Marie. "He wasn't in our way; you saw that for yourself, and he still looked so worn out."

"His comrades are waiting for him," Madame Sellier said firmly. "Besides, he's right; the house is no longer safe. The Germans will realize one of these days that Monsieur Jean had nothing to do with that affair and, who knows?—they may come back here to look for Alain. . . . By the way, what are we going to do with the typewriter? It was used to type out underground assignments. If the Germans later find one of those papers and search the house, they may recognize the type. We must anticipate everything. Where are we going to hide it?"

The concierge was consulted. She suggested that the typewriter be taken to her cousin, who lived in the neighborhood. They would later explain the whole matter to Monsieur Jean . . . that is, if he ever came back.

Madame Sellier returned to her apartment. She kept thinking of Solange. What would the poor little thing say when she learned that her brother had left without seeing her again? She didn't dare tell her this.

Solange's condition improved despite everything. But she was so weak when she got up from bed for the first time that she was barely able to take a few steps across the room. Doctor Ménard prescribed injections, which he came to administer every other day. So many visits! Madame Sellier was worried—how would she ever be able to pay such a large sum? And she reluctantly spoke to the doctor about his fees during one of his visits.

"Don't worry about it!" he said, not even letting her finish what she was going to say, and adding, "What about all the concern and trouble you have taken? Let's say that the two of us are sharing the care of this child, and let's not talk about money any more."

On New Year's Eve there was another bombing raid by the English, which destroyed a munitions factory at Courbevoie. Solange was still bedridden. Madame Sellier stayed in the apartment with her and sent the children down to the shelter in the care of the Moscots. At each explosion, the little girl stared at the vibrating windows and shrank in her arms with fright. It was that evening, as the bombs fell, that Madame Sellier realized clearly what she would have to do. She would have to keep Solange with them till the end of the war. There was no other solution.

Fanfan's Teddy Bear

Toward the middle of January there finally was news of Monsieur Jean. A short, bearded, hollow-cheeked man called on the concierge one morning. He explained that he had recently been released from the Fresnes detention camp, and that for two weeks Monsieur Jean had been his cellmate. The young man asked him to inform his neighbors that the Germans had finally realized their mistake and had decided to set him free. But days had passed and he was still waiting. Could they possibly send him some clean clothes and food?

The whole house got busy at once. Madame Queline mended his shirts and socks, and everyone searched once more through what remained in their bureau drawers. When the parcel was ready, the Minet sisters, who had felt useless since Alain's departure, volunteered to take it to the prisoner. Madame Sellier now remembered a remark Doctor Ménard had made to her during one of his visits. Didn't he say that he had "connections" at Fresnes? She spoke to him about Monsieur Jean's plight next time he came to give Solange an injection.

"Yes, indeed, I could see your friend," he said, "and I might even be able to do more than that. Just between us, I know the German who is in charge of the prison records—a sorry specimen who would do anything for money—I have had some dealings with him. If you give him three thousand francs, he'll put the folder of your prisoner on top of the others, and the thing will be done. Believe me," he went on, "it is necessary to take some action or your Monsieur Jean may rot there till the end of the war. And worse, they may deport him to Germany."

"But, since they have admitted that . . ."

"Would that necessarily make any difference to them? Resister or not, Monsieur Jean is a man, a man who may sooner or later involve himself in some action against them, and as long as he remains in their clutches . . ."

"Then," Madame Sellier said decisively, "we'll proceed."

The residents of the house now had to raise three thousand francs, somehow. The doctor contributed five hundred, the Moscots one thousand, the old ladies eight hundred—which they took from their small savings—and Madame Sellier, after carefully going over her accounts, thought she could spare two hundred francs. The rest was supplied by Monsieur Lampion and the concierge.

And two days later Monsieur Jean was a free man. He showed up toward evening, dirty, haggard, unkempt. He announced right off that he would not speak to anyone before he made himself presentable. That took him quite a long time, but when he finally emerged from his place, he looked better groomed than ever, despite his sallow complexion. He came up to the Sellier apartment, where the tenants had gathered to hear his story. He greeted them one by one, adjusting his tie after each handshake.

"Come on, let's hear what happened," they said. Everyone was eager to know.

"Well," he began, "I acted the fool to perfection. Nevertheless that didn't seem to bother them much, and at first they treated me fairly decently. 'Are you Alain Couture?' they asked. 'Alain Couture?' I replied. 'Of course not—my name is *Jean-Felix Parizot!*' 'But you know Alain Couture?' 'Yes, he is a neighbor of mine. We sometimes meet on the stairs, but that's all. . . . By the way, I have a cousin whose name is *Aline Voiture*,' I added. 'Perhaps you got her name confused with his?' Then they questioned me endlessly about the Résistance and wanted to know if I would work against the maquis. I feigned utter astonishment at such an idea. 'When would I have the time?' I asked. 'I have enough to do at my pharmacy!' I said. 'And as far as the Résistance is concerned, I know they exist, of course, but nothing more!' Whereupon the Germans chuckled—with disbelief, I suppose—nudged each other, and told me that they were going to let me go. But instead of freeing me they sent me off to Fresnes. You can't imagine what goes on over there!" Monsieur Jean recalled with bitter indignation. "Would you believe it! Imagine!—a big lumpy fellow was going to help himself to my tie! '*Selbstbinder*' he bellowed, pulling at my neck. Then bang! A slap, another! At this point one of them intervened and explained to me that the one who had hit me wanted my tie. I exploded, 'Couldn't you have explained more clearly what you wanted instead of slugging me?' I took off my tie. But you have no idea. . . ."

"And what else went on there?" asked the concierge. "In the cells, for instance?"

"It wouldn't have been so bad if I hadn't been dying of hunger all the time. There were two others with me, the short, bearded man whom you have met and a Breton whom they shipped off to Germany, yesterday. If you only knew all the tricks that the prisoners resort to over there! They hide all kinds of things in the mattresses—a knife, paper, pencils. And the amazing system of tapping on the walls to communicate with the prisoners in other cells! The hardest time was in the evening, because we had no light. We stretched out in the dark and tried to converse, but soon we fell silent. In fact, we would sleep most of the time. In the morning some of the prisoners were taken out and driven away in a truck—we knew they were the men who were going to be shot! And we all sang the 'Marseillaise'. . . ."

"And were they actually shot?" exclaimed Mademoiselle Marie, wringing her hands.

"I don't know. . . . Very likely, since they never came back. . . . Every other day they carted off some of the men that way, and every other day we sang. . . . When they freed the bearded one, I asked him to come and see you. Thank you all very much for the parcel," added Monsieur Jean politely.

Madame Sellier asked, "When did they interrogate you? What day was it, exactly?"

"Wait . . . let me see . . . I was arrested on the twenty-fourth, they kept me two days at the local precinct on Rue des Saussaies. That means I must have been questioned on the twenty-sixth. But why do you ask?"

"The twenty-sixth . . ." repeated Madame Sellier.

"That's the day when the spy disappeared from across the street. They must have understood by then that you weren't Alain and therefore stopped watching the house. That means that Alain was not followed when he left."

"How fortunate!" cried the Minet ladies.

Then they told Monsieur Jean about Doctor Ménard's help, saying nothing about the three thousand francs. "So I owe my freedom to him? What a kind person he must be—I'll pay him a visit to thank him," he said. Then he suddenly declared: "Let me tell you—I'm not going to stay in any safe little corner from now on. They disgust me too much, those Nazi swine, with their trucks full of men they send every morning to their death! I've sung the 'Marseillaise' too often recently to remain aloof. . . . Besides, how they dealt with me! slapping me, helping themselves to my tie! Oh no, I don't want to stay in my safe little corner any longer—I want to fight . . . and if I can be of any help to Alain . . ."

"Right now the first thing you must do is put on a little weight," said Madame Sellier with a smile. "Have dinner with us tonight."

"No, with us!" said Monsieur Moscot.

Monsieur Jean dined with the Selliers. Next day he had lunch with the Moscots and dinner with the spinster sisters. He was welcome with everyone. And Madame Queline was satisfied with her tenants, indeed she was proud of them. They all faced up to the enemy, all of them—from the top floor to the bottom! When her son returned and told her about his brave deeds, she too would have things to tell him!

But there remained one black stain on the reputation of her house: the Gourres. Could it have been they who had informed on Alain? Again and again the tenants made inquiries, trying to find out. Michel and George kept putting questions to Stéphane, this way and that way, without of course disclosing their purpose. But Stéphane always answered them with double talk. The Gourres, guilty or not, guarded their secret well.

"It *was* the Gourres!" Michel confided in George. "I know it! How could it have been anyone else? My opinion is that they should be told to their faces what they have done. Then they should be kicked out of the house."

George shrugged. "That would be impossible. It couldn't be done before Victory. When that comes, all kinds of things will happen. Just wait and see!"

The winter holidays were over now. The two boys had returned to school, and Michel tried to work harder at his studies. He had turned over to George his leadership in the league, and the Pirates were limiting their activities to slipping leaflets into the neighborhood mailboxes. The league, the green leaflets—it all no longer interested Michel. He could think only of Daniel. But he had not heard from him since the day he first met him at the *Rendez-Vous*. Could it be that Daniel had forgotten his promise? . . .

One morning in February, as Michel was crossing the Luxembourg Gardens, slushing in the melting snow, he ran into Alain. He hardly recognized him. Alain was no longer blond—he now had dark-brown hair; he wore a broad-brimmed felt hat and glasses.

"I've been looking for you," the young man said. "I didn't want to go near the Rue des Quatre-Vents, so I've been hanging around near your school. In fact, I was on my way there now. Daniel needs you."

Michel's face flushed crimson.

"At last!" he cried. "Tell me, quick, what do I do?"

"You have to take a message *today* to a cleaning establishment on Rue Guénégaud. You'll ask to speak to a Mademoiselle Agathe. You'll tell her: 'Martin sent me,' and you'll give her this."

Michel slipped the scrap of paper inside his shirt. This, by now familiar gesture, made him thrill with excitement.

"That isn't all," Alain said to him. "You'll come back here next Tuesday, at four o'clock, and I'll give you a second message. Don't forget—it's next Tuesday at four." Alain lit a cigarette and left, his feet splashing through the unavoidable puddles.

Michel hesitated a moment. He couldn't go on that kind of errand without first telling his mother. But ought he tell her the truth? What if she wouldn't let him go to Rue Guénéguad? "Well, it will be too bad if she doesn't," he told himself, "but I can't hide this sort of thing from her." He went home to tell her.

Madame Sellier listened, sighed, and in the end murmured, "Go ahead, son."

Michel located the place without trouble and carried out his mission faithfully. To do this he had to miss school that day. He was absent from school again three days later, when Alain sent him much farther, to Belleville. The young blonde whom he had met a month earlier was waiting for him at the Métro exit at Places des Fêtes. She stood there, pretending to read her newspaper. She sent him on to Ternes, to Maillot, to Vaugirard, to Rue La Fayette. At each place—at street corners or in shops—he contacted people whose names he didn't know. But as soon as he said "Martin," they looked at him searchingly and received his message. Gradually he gained confidence. And he was more cautious this time. When he passed a German on the street, he refrained from sneering—this was hardly the time to be noticed or arrested, while working for the Résistance, he reasoned.

One Thursday afternoon, as he was on his way back to school after lunch, he met Alain behind the Panthéon building. "Today it's a bit more complicated," the young man said. "This time you won't be delivering anything. You'll bring something back to us—a plan, or rather an outline of a plan, which we must act on this very evening. The place you must go to is quite far from here, at Saint-Rémy-lès-Chevreuse, out in the suburbs. I would have preferred to assign this task to someone else, but we have no one right now, and it is urgent. Do you think you could do it?"

"Yes, Monsieur Alain."

"Good! You'll take the train at the Luxembourg depot, get off at Saint-Rémy—that's the end of the line—and you'll look for a sewing materials store with the sign *Desvignes*. The store is painted green on the outside. There will be an old woman behind the counter. After making sure that she is Madame Desvignes, you'll give the password. She'll give you the plan."

"And what do I do with it?"

"You will take it to Daniel. He will be waiting for you at the *Rendez-Vous* café, until six o'clock."

"Daniel! . . ." Michel stammered. "Will I really see Daniel?"

"Really! And does that mean so much to you? . . . I

guess it's not surprising. Daniel . . . Anyway, you'll see him, my friend! Now then, do you have some money? No? . . . Here is one hundred francs. I don't have any change. You must hurry. There is a train around two o'clock."

It was already one-forty. If he ran, he'd have just enough time to go home to tell his mother, then make that two o'clock train.

When he finally found himself on the train, he caught his breath and was at last able to relax and enjoy his good luck. He was going to see Daniel! Daniel would talk to him! He, Michel, would answer him! How long the afternoon was going to seem—six o'clock would never come! He thought the train wasn't moving fast enough, that nothing would happen fast enough till that hour. He trembled with impatience. From the corner of the compartment where he sat, he looked out on the passing houses and streets without seeing them.

Then he happened to put his hand in his pocket and felt something soft. It was Fanfan's teddy bear. He had had a spat with his little brother before breakfast. Fanfan had taken his eraser and Michel, to get even, had grabbed Nono, which he had hidden in his pocket. So now he still had the toy bear, having forgotten in his haste to return it to Fanfan. That was stupid—what was *he* doing with a teddy bear—him, Daniel's personal courier! Michel felt like throwing the thing out the window, but knowing that Fanfan would be very upset, he hid it inside his handkerchief instead, still feeling annoyed with himself.

The train pulled in at Saint-Rémy. Michel darted out onto the platform, left the station, and looked around for the green store. He noticed it soon, on the left, at the end of a long, narrow street. He walked toward it, humming. The air was bracing, and the wind, smelling of the country, blew hard. It reminded Michel of his grandmother's orchard and the woods that surrounded it. Next summer he'd build a shed, and in the future he wouldn't let Norette climb on anything he built. That girl surely liked to climb on everything! Then he suddenly remembered where he was and why—what was he thinking of, daydreaming like that! He entered the store.

An old, white-haired woman, with spectacles astride her nose, was sitting at the cash register. Seeing Michel, she took off her glasses and asked him pleasantly what he wanted. Michel gave the password. The old woman's face clouded.

"All right," she said, looking uneasily through the window. "Wait here."

She disappeared through a small door and soon returned with a sheet of transparent paper. It was folded so many times that it looked like a small, round wad in her hand.

"It isn't big," she whispered, "but I rolled it on purpose, as a precaution. I have the feeling that I'm being watched. Warn Martin, will you? Now, let's see, where will you put it?"

"What? . . ." said Michel. "I don't really know. It's so small, I'm afraid I might lose it. In my change purse, maybe? . . ."

"Really?—so that they find it right away? Don't you know that's the first thing they look into when they search you! And don't forget—if you are arrested, you will expose me, too . . . and that doesn't appeal to me at all! It's bad enough having all those Germans prowl around my place! . . . Well? Where are you going to put it?"

"I have an idea," Michel said. He slipped behind the register so as not to be visible from the outside, took Nono out of his pocket, and examined the toy for a moment. "Do you have a pair of scissors?" he asked.

With the point of the scissors he enlarged the socket of Nono's missing eye and pushed the wad into it with his finger.

"That's clever," said the old woman, "but don't go and lose your bear, whatever you do. Put it way down in your pocket." Then she added with a sigh, "You seem to me like a nice kid. What a job they've wished on you! . . . Wait, my poor boy, I'm going to give you a little something."

She took several boxes from a case, rummaged through them, and offered Michel a blue pencil.

"Thank you, madame," the thrilled Michel said. "I'll use it to color rivers with."

He was so excited about the pencil that he took the wrong way back to the station, turning into a dirty, dead-end street strewn with loose cobblestones. He was retracing his steps, furious with himself, when suddenly he stopped, aghast. A German in a green uniform (a Gestapo man) had stationed himself at the head of the street, barring Michel's way. "If I run the other way," Michel thought, "he'll know that I'm afraid of him. So, forward march! Maybe he'll go away." But the German didn't budge. When Michel was about to pass him, he put his hand heavily on his shoulder. Michel trembled at the contact.

"Where you . . . to go?" asked the soldier, pronouncing the French words with difficulty.

"I'm going back to Paris," answered Michel. "I'm on my way to the station."

"Where you to come from? Why you to go to the woman . . . Desvignes?"

Michel bit his lip. So, the German had followed him, and that meant the old woman wasn't mistaken—her store was under surveillance.

"I went there to buy a . . . a . . ." he stammered, taking the pencil out of his pocket, ". . . a pencil."

The German snickered and didn't comment. He grabbed Michel by the arm. "Come along," he said, still snickering and adding in German, "*mit mir* . . . with me!"

Michel veered around, and measured from the corner of his eye the distance that separated him from the cross street. It was only a few yards, and once there . . . He lurched forward, trying to tear himself away, but he didn't succeed in getting free from his captor's grip. The soldier shook him and smacked him on the head with his large open hand. "*Mit mir.* . . . You understand?"

Michel followed him, his heart pounding. He was so outraged that he didn't even think of being afraid. Besides, to let himself be trapped that way, like an idiot! "Like a stupid idiot!" he kept muttering. "And what will Daniel say when he hears about this? He'll be waiting and waiting for me. He'll think me a nincompoop. . . . And if they find that thing—the paper—no, they're too stupid for that!" He pushed his hand deep into his pocket and held the little bear tightly in his fist.

The German marched alongside of him, never once turning his head. A few tense faces peered through windows and immediately disappeared. A young woman holding an infant looked at them in silence as they passed. They crossed one street, entered another—a deserted one—and finally stopped in front of a gray building bearing the sign: *Kommandantur*—military police station. The soldier opened the door and pushed Michel into a small, dirty-walled, overheated room. Behind a table full of folders sat the officer in charge—obese, greasy, with a bloated face, his bald head covered with beads of sweat; he was smoking a cigar. Another German, his back to the fireplace and notepad in hand, was taking notes.

The soldier pulled Michel toward the table, clicked his heels, and made his report mechanically. The officer raised his head and fixed his pale eyes on Michel.

"Come closer," he commanded. And when Michel didn't move, the officer bellowed, taking the cigar from his mouth, "*Treten sie herein!* Approach!" The soldier pushed Michel forward with a sharp blow on his back.

Michel braced himself and stood erect in front of the table, making a great effort not to tremble.

"How your name? Your address?"

"Sellier, Michel, 24 Rue des Quatre-Vents, Paris."

"What does your father?"

"My father is a prisoner in Germany," answered the son, proudly.

"Ah, *ja, ja* . . . yes, yes . . . Give me what you have in your hand."

Michel put the blue pencil on the table.

"Is that all?"

The officer gestured to the soldier. The soldier pinned back Michel's arms and began to go through his pockets.

He found the change purse, a handkerchief, the teddy bear.

"The . . . how do you call it . . . sweater," barked the bald officer.

Michel took off his sweater. The rough hands frisked him, raised his shirt. He felt their damp touch on his skin, but his attention centered on Nono. The interrogating officer had grabbed Nono by its paw, looking intently at its empty socket. One moment, two moments passed. Michel waited, shaking. Suddenly the officer flung the bear across the table with disgust. Nono landed near the fire, at the feet of the German with the notepad. "Good!" Michel said to himself. "He didn't notice anything, the blockhead!" He was seized with a mad desire to laugh, barely managing to control himself.

"*Nichts* . . . Nothing . . ." said the soldier when he finished searching Michel, and stood at attention.

The officer shrugged, put the cigar back in his mouth, and began to roll the blue pencil over the table, the wheels obviously turning in his head. "You have bought it from the woman Desvignes?" he asked at last, pointing to the pencil.

"Yes," answered Michel. "I already said that."

"And the woman Desvignes has gave you nothing else? You not brought anything to her either?"

"No, nothing."

The officer half closed his pale eyes, and his face assumed a phony kindly expression. "It's very bad to lie, very bad. You didn't come all the long way from Paris just to buy a pencil. What will he say, your papa in Germany, when he finds out that his son did lied?"

"My dad . . ." sputtered Michel, turning scarlet. He

took hold of himself and continued in a firm voice, "I didn't come to this town only for that, I also came to try to find some meat, because they didn't have any in our market. Mother sent me here, because it's Thursday and school is out today. She gave me one hundred francs—you can see for yourself, the bill is in my change purse!"

"That's very bad," repeated the officer, as if he had not heard a word of what Michel had just said.

Then he blew out a spiral of smoke and added, stressing each word, "You know what we do with liars? We shoot them!" And he made the gesture of cocking an imaginary rifle. "You do not want us to shoot you, now would you? That is going to make your mother very unhappy, no?"

Michel didn't answer him. He kept staring at the officer's moist and red mouth, which was puckered around his cigar. "You're not scaring me, you foul Fritz," he said to himself. "Talk, talk, talk, always talk . . . too bad there isn't any rat poison in your cigar!"

The officer stroked his bald pate. "So, you're not going to tell us nothing?" he asked. "Then we shoot you!"

And he smiled his "kindly" smile again. Michel winced. Was it true? Were they going to kill him?

"But I can't die," he thought desperately, ". . . if I die, Daniel won't get the plan, and I promised Alain, I promised . . ." Tears choked him. He wanted to appeal to the bald officer, feeling at the same time like striking that sallow face, those pale eyes looking at him with such maddening placidity. "Dirty dog!" he murmured. "Dirty dog!" But already he was being pulled away by the soldier. His eyes swept the small room for the last time—he saw the pencil on the table and Nono still lying near the fireplace. "Oh, no!" he thought. "I'm not going to leave Nono here. They are not going to have a chance to find the paper after I'm dead!" He bent down quickly, freeing himself from the soldier's grip, and ran to pick up the teddy bear.

"*Ach.*" The officer grinned. "You're taking your bear with you? Good, they're going to shoot you together. . . . Now, get out of here!"

This time Michel offered no resistance. He was so glad to have outsmarted the Germans that he hardly thought of what was in store for him. When he got outside, however, all this changed. The soldier led him into a garden surrounded by low walls. There were four soldiers in the garden, rifles in hand. They were standing at attention near a flight of stairs. The soldier shouted a few words to them, casting a puzzling look at Michel. He pushed Michel against the wall and snarled an order. The four rifles were immediately aimed at Michel. He stiffened. "I'm not afraid. . . . I'm not afraid. . . . I'm not afraid . . ." he kept repeating to himself in order to gain courage, but the black holes of the gun barrels terrified him. One . . . Two . . . Three . . . Four . . . Was it going to be very painful? He recalled the time he had fallen downstairs and hit his forehead, making it bleed. He remembered that he hadn't cried, and his mother . . . "Mother! . . ." he now cried out, barely holding back the tears. "But, they will not get that paper!" he murmured through his dry lips. He closed his eyes and gripped Nono in his hand, pressing the toy desperately to his side.

A minute passed, a minute which seemed to last forever. The Germans did not fire. Michel opened his eyes gradually. What were they waiting for? And why hadn't they tied his hands, as they do in storybooks? The effort that he was making to stand erect against that wall was draining all his strength, and he felt sick to his stomach. "Why don't they get it over with!" he said to himself fiercely. "Why don't they shoot! I can't stand this any more!"

The four Germans lowered their rifles and burst into guffaws of laughter. His captor, advancing a step, pointed with his finger to the flight of stairs.

"*Ach!* You can go, little *Franzose*—little Frenchman!"

Warily, Michel moved away from the wall. He saw black. He stumbled up the stairs blindly. His legs shook and he staggered. But when he finally reached the door to the street, when at last he realized fully that he was indeed free, a deep shudder went through him and he broke into sobs—the violent sobs of a child, shaking him to the depths of his being. "Mother!" he moaned. "Oh, Mother!" And he suddenly felt a desperate need to see his mother again, to be close to her, to have her comfort him. Then he remembered that Daniel was waiting for him. Swallowing his tears, Michel glanced at Nono and moved on toward the station, running in spurts, when he had the strength for it.

The train for Paris had begun to move out of the station. It was almost empty of passengers. Michel climbed aboard and sat down in a corner seat. How soft and comfortable that seat was! How smoothly the train rolled along. How contented the people around him seemed to be! Everything looked and felt wonderful to him! He noticed through the train window a little girl on a garden swing, and he wished he knew her and could play with her.

But another thought suddenly took possession of him, making him freeze with terror! What if that bald officer had had him followed in order to find out where he'd go? He looked around anxiously at the passengers—a portly gentleman, a short young man in a gray overcoat, a woman in blue, another in black. The portly man seemed to be looking straight at him. Yes, he was certainly staring at him. . . . Michel turned his eyes away, overcome with fear. He had thought he was finally safe, but now he was in danger again. The thought shocked and unsettled him. He had no idea what he should do now. He wished he could remain sitting on that bench and never have to leave the train. But Daniel! He had to get to Daniel. Before six o'clock. But first he had to escape the attention of the fat man. He forced himself to think calmly and clearly, and with great difficulty decided on a plan of subterfuge.

When the train pulled into the Luxembourg depot, Michel left the station and walked across the Place de Medici. He forced himself not to look around, but when he reached the opposite side of the square he cautiously looked back from the corner of his eye, hardly turning his head. The stout man was nowhere to be seen, but it was the young man in the gray overcoat who was following him. This one or the other, it came to the same thing. There was no other way out—he had to carry out that plan. By now he was so worn out that he had to use superhuman will power not to give up and go directly home. The whole thing was too much for him, he couldn't go on with it!

But Michel braced himself somehow. He walked as fast as he could toward his school, on Rue Vaugirard. He rang the bell and explained to the custodian that he had forgotten his arithmetic book in his desk the previous day, and that he had come to get it so as to be able to do his homework. He then walked to his classroom and waited there for ten whole minutes, his eyes on the clock. It was exactly five o'clock when he cautiously left the school building, crossed the playground, and slipped out the door used for deliveries. This door opened onto the corner. He looked around and realized that he had succeeded in shaking off the short young man! His heart beat so fast by now that it hurt him to breathe. Nevertheless, he felt a strong urge to sing the "Marseillaise," like Monsieur Jean. Then, upon entering the Métro his spirits sank again: all those people he would brush against; all those faces that would seem to be watching him. No, it would be better to go on foot all the way to the *Rendez-Vous*. He left the subway and jogged toward the Seine, his legs barely able to move, his head feverish. He trembled all over and didn't dare look at anyone. He reached the Carrousel bridge, then the Avenue de l'Opéra, next the Rue de Rome . . . five-thirty . . . five-forty . . . five-forty-five . . . Would he get to Daniel in time? When he finally turned into the Rue Boursault, he was feeling faint and everything was spinning around him. He continued doggedly, dragging his weary feet step after step. Finally he was in the café. He looked so deathly pale that Daniel, seeing him, was alarmed.

"You look awful! What's happened to you? I began to think you wouldn't come!"

"I . . . I . . ." Michel could hardly speak. What's more, he felt that he would burst out crying if he said another word. So he contented himself with raising his eyes to Daniel, expressing in them everything he wanted to say. Daniel pushed a half-full glass toward him. "Drink this," he said.

It was whisky and lemon juice. The drink warmed his insides; his heart calmed down; and he could breathe more easily. "I was arrested," he began, "when I left the Desvignes store. . . ."

Daniel listened to the whole account, his head lowered, as was his manner, and he showed no emotion. When Michel had finished, he said dryly, "So, another 'mail box' gone; I think Madame Desvignes understands that she has to go into hiding now. As for you," he went on more feelingly, "I doubt that they had you tailed after they let you go—they must have believed your story. Do you feel better now? . . . Let me have that paper."

Michel took Nono from his pocket, poked his finger into the socket, and pulled out the small wad. Daniel unfolded it carefully and put it in his wallet. Then he looked at Michel approvingly, and said, "Well done!"

And Michel felt that the terrible hours he had just lived through, the menacing Germans, their fiendish joke with the rifles, his terror and loneliness—all seemed not to matter, now that Daniel had said those two words to him.

George

Michel didn't tell his mother about the dangers of his mission, nor did he cling to her, as he had so desperately craved to do when he got clear of the *Kommandantur*. When he reached home, he found her in such a state of worry that he fully realized, for the first time, how much his errands for the Résistance cost her, how hard it all was on her health. He decided to spare her the truth of that afternoon's events. Nor did he speak of it to George.

What had happened remained a secret between Daniel and himself, a secret that brought them closer and that Michel guarded jealously in his heart. As he was leaving, Daniel had told him that for the time being he would not send him out with any more messages. Since the Germans now knew his address, it would be wiser for Michel not to have any contact with the group for a while.

Michel had resigned himself to the "sentence," but he couldn't help counting the weeks with growing impatience. Now it was March. Tiny leaves were sprouting on the chestnut trees in the Luxembourg Gardens, but there still was no sign of Alain or the blond girl.

Solange, too, was despondent. Why hadn't she received any word from her brother? To calm her fears, Madame Sellier decided to tell the little girl that Alain had to remain in hiding somewhere in the countryside and that it wasn't safe for him to write. "But, just a few words," Solange kept saying to her. "If he'd only write a few words, like 'I'm all right,' that would make me so happy—if I got just those three short words!" And Solange continued to hang around the concierge's door every morning, waiting for the mailman.

"Is there nothing for me, Madame Queline?" The concierge would shake her head, and Solange would leave despondently for school. With each day she became thinner and paler, despite the injections that Doctor Ménard kept giving her regularly.

The spring brought great news, however. Unleashing a big offensive, the Russians were attacking the Germans on the Baltic. A fierce battle was raging there. The Nazis, pressed on all sides, were retreating to new positions. And the German Chief of Staff termed the retreats and routs of his armies "a complete defensive victory." The Anglo-American invasion of the shores of France was expected any day. Would they invade from the north? Or from the south? Each prediction had its staunch followers. At the same time that the Germans were fortifying the French coastline, they were assuring the French people that the promised Allied invasion "was nothing but a big bluff."

The Fritzes could be seen in the restaurants listening

to the radio, their arms resting on the tables; and the plates full of sausages in front of them remained uneaten.

The French people passing the restaurants would look at each other and exchange meaningful smiles. And everyone kept gazing with intense and secret joy at the tiny black dots in the sky, the English bombers way up above the clouds, gliding in formations of five, toward the south. The air-raid alerts increased in frequency, meat and vegetables disappeared from the marketstalls, but no one complained, since the end of the war was near.

Every evening the small dining room at the Selliers was crowded with neighbors. Old man Lampion, Monsieur Jean, the Moscots, the demoiselles Minet, the concierge—they all came to listen to the English broadcasts. The evening when the liberation of the Russian city of Odessa was announced, grandfather Lampion treated the gathering to a bottle of white wine. And in celebration of the American invasion of Italy, south of Rome, the Minet ladies baked a prune pie; it was exactly like the one they had contributed to the Christmas Eve dinner. Things certainly had changed for the better since that night.

The occupants of the house now laughed up their sleeves whenever they thought of the Gourres. Feeling uneasy and ashamed, the collaborationists kept assuring whoever would listen that they never despised the English. The German officer, who used to visit them to guzzle and stuff himself with food, had left for the Russian front, but no one had replaced him to partake of the "hospitality" of the Gourres. Realizing that the wind was blowing the other way, they were ready to make a complete about-face. But they didn't take into account their son Stéphane. They had allowed and encouraged him to cry "Heil Hitler!" and to follow enthusiastically the evil route of German victories for the past four years. Now they were reaping the results—he had become a full-fledged Nazi and remained one with all the fanaticism of his twelve years. His parents' false shift of loyalty filled him with contempt, and he regarded them as cowards. In his general resentment he kept beating up his little brother Louis, who now refused to share his allegiance to the Germans.

There were constant arguments at school among the children. The band of Pirates had grown in numbers. Big Bobin and a dozen other schoolboys had joined the league, and the leaflets written by *Leonidas* (George), full of calls to victory, were flooding the neighborhood. These young patriots no longer had to remain silent and watch out for Stéphane's sleuthing. In fact, they now showered Stéphane with jeers, asking him for the latest "news about Hitler." Stéphane smiled a crooked smile and said that he had reliable information that the *Führer* (he pronounced the word in the German way) would win in the end—that he wasn't yet at the "end of his rope." George then scoffed at the young Hitlerite, advising him "to warn his hero that the rope might snap any day, and, then, what a tumble!" The boys laughed uproariously; Stéphane was livid with rage and gritted his teeth, repeating that the "rope would hold."

One May morning following one such argument, George was walking home from school. He was in good spirits. Michel was with him. Stéphane was following them several paces behind. The two friends were deliberately laughing very hard to taunt Stéphane. They were only talking about Bobin and Ménard, and the history composition which they would be writing in class the next day.

A tall, awkward boy with a thin, long nose stopped abruptly as he was passing the two chatting boys.

"Hi, there, Moskowitz!" he called out. "Do you live in Paris now?"

George looked at him, nodded his head in greeting, and continued on his way without answering the other's question. The tall boy turned around and followed him. "Say, don't you recognize me? I'm Dulong–I was in your class in Lyons! You remember . . . Father Trequet . . . you and me playing billiards . . . you swiping my cap . . ."

"Ah, yes," George answered vaguely. "Excuse me, I'm in a hurry. Good-by!"

The other boy made a face, being half puzzled and half offended. George increased his pace.

"Don't you remember him?" asked Michel.

"Yes, I do. . . . What an imbecile!–to call me *Moskowitz* here, outside, right in the street! Do you think Stéphane heard him, there behind us?"

"You're right," said Michel. "It didn't occur to me at first. . . . Wait . . ."

He veered around to take Stéphane by surprise. He saw him loiter at the window of a millinery shop, looking at the display of women's hats.

"He is looking at women's hats!" Michel whispered, giggling. "Can you imagine that?–women's hats! At least it proves that he didn't hear anything."

"Hmm!" said George doubtfully. "I wish I could be certain. It seems suspicious to me that he is suddenly taking such an interest in those hats. . . . Now, don't say anything to my mother. Especially not to her. It would make her worry herself sick! What a moron that Dulong is!" Then George forced himself to talk about something else.

Michel soon forgot the incident. The next day, coming home from school, where he had done his history composition passably well, he found little Louis waiting for him in front of the house. "I want to tell you something," Louis whispered, looking worried, "but not here —let's go somewhere else."

He led Michel a little farther up the block. They stopped near the entrance to another building. After first looking carefully down the street, he whispered into Michel's ear, speaking very fast, "Stéphane has informed on George."

"What?" cried the stunned Michel.

"Oh, please!" Louis begged. "Don't shout! He might hear us!—if Stéphane finds out that I told you, he'll be furious, just furious!"

"But . . ." stammered Michel, "that's impossible!"

"No, it's true. He did inform on him . . . to the Germans! He said that he did it because you made him so mad, in school, and that it would serve you all right. . . . You see, yesterday morning he heard someone call George by a different name . . . a Jewish name."

"George isn't Jewish . . ." Michel protested weakly.

"Stéphane says he is. He says that he has a Jewish name, that 'Moscot' isn't his real name. It was because of all this that I've been waiting in the street for you. I don't care about Monsieur Couture, but a schoolmate—that's different!"

"So!" said Michel, gritting his teeth. "So it's *he* who betrayed Alain?"

Louis' lips quivered and he was about to cry. "I didn't mean to tell you that—the words slipped out," he whimpered. "I didn't want to tell you, and it just slipped out. Please don't tell anyone! Don't ever repeat to anyone what I just told you, please!"

"You needn't worry," Michel said to him, "and thanks for the information. Now you wait here—it's better for us not to be seen together. Let me go first."

Michel rushed upstairs and, badly shaken, told the news to his mother. "I've been expecting something like this to happen," Madame Sellier said in a woebegone voice. "Oh, my God! Those poor people, what are they going to do? I'd better warn them right away!"

The Moscots were just sitting down to dinner when Madame Sellier came in. Seeing her look so pale, Monsieur Moscot guessed everything. "Someone has informed on us," he murmured.

Madame Sellier nodded, and she went over to George's mother who was looking at her with bewilderment.

"It was Stéphane," cried George. "I knew he heard everything yesterday. . . . And Michel said that he didn't!"

"Heard what?" his father asked.

And George told them about yesterday's encounter with Dulong.

"He's right," Madame Sellier said. "It was Stéphane."

"Now they're going to arrest us!" moaned Madame Moscot, crushed with grief. "They're going to take away my boy!"

She was gasping for breath. Her husband, beside himself with fear, burst out, "Be still, woman! Don't you realize how unbearable it is to listen to you carry on like this at a time when we must make immediate plans! . . . But . . . what plans?" he asked miserably, his voice trailing off as he covered his eyes with his hand. "We must leave this place within minutes . . . but where can we go? Where?"

"I've wondered about that," said Madame Sellier. "I think you could hide out at my mother's, in Allier; it's a very small village, near Montluçon. I think you'll be safe there."

"In Allier?" Madame Moscot repeated in a tear-choked voice. "We'd have to take the train—they'd ask us for our papers, and they'd arrest us!"

Madame Sellier took the woman's trembling hand and held it between hers. "Not at all," she said gently. "Don't worry, they will not arrest you. I thought of that possibility, too; of course you must obtain false papers, and I think Monsieur Lampion would be able to help you. Judging by what he says goes on at his printing shop, that should be possible. I'll speak to him about it this very evening."

"If you speak to him this evening," said Monsieur Moscot, "he wouldn't have them for us before tomorrow, at the earliest, and between now and then . . ."

And, indeed, between now and then, what were the Moscots going to do? It was impossible to hide them in the building, for the Germans might search the other apartments, as they had done Christmas Eve when they were after Alain Couture. Madame Sellier finally suggested that they send George over to Monsieur Planquet, her husband's former employer; he was a man you could depend on, and luckily his little daughter had left that day to spend some time with one of her aunts. George could sleep in her room. As for Monsieur and Madame Moscot, why couldn't they go to stay with the concierge's cousin, the one who was keeping the typewriter for Monsieur Jean. Surely she wouldn't refuse to give them shelter for the next few days.

"All right, if you think we should," said Monsieur Moscot, adding, "Madame Sellier, it never fails—you are always at hand when there are people to be saved! First Alain . . . then Monsieur Jean . . . and now it is our turn. . . ."

"Nonsense! Wouldn't you do as much for me?" she said, forcing a smile.

She went down and sent Norette to forewarn the concierge. Madame Queline came up at once, without even stopping to roll down her sleeves, which she had pushed up to do a wash. When she heard in detail what had happened, she cursed the Gourres and assured the Moscots that her cousin would be "glad to help those who otherwise would fall into the enemy's clutches." So it was decided that George should leave first and that Michel would accompany him and explain to Monsieur Planquet what help was expected of him. Madame Moscot packed some linen and clothes into a small suitcase for him. But when everything was ready, when she had to take leave of her son, she was overcome with despair, clinging to him and covering his face with kisses, as if she were never going to see him again.

"Mother, let me go!" George finally said, freeing himself from her embrace. "Everyone will think I'm a baby. I'm twelve, you know!"

"And since he's leaving us for only a couple of days . . ." added Monsieur Moscot, his voice faltering. "Go now, son, go along with Michel," he said.

George grabbed his valise and left without looking back.

His mother sank into a chair, grieving, "I'll never see him again!"

"Of course you'll see him again," said Madame Queline. "And what about me? . . . I haven't held my son in my arms for a whole year! But this is certainly no time for chatting. Better let me give you a hand with the rest of the packing."

It wasn't so simple to do that, however. Madame Moscot was distraught. She couldn't keep her mind on what had to be done. She'd look for a shirt here, pick up a tie there, unable to decide what to pack. Again and again they had to take from her hands the books that George had been awarded as prizes for his excellence in school. She insisted on taking them along. Following her around her husband pleaded that she hurry. He finally had to warn her that she would indeed never see George again if they didn't leave soon. This argument prevailed. Madame Moscot somehow regained her composure, and they soon left. The stricken woman was helped down the stairs by Madame Sellier. The concierge walked ahead of them to make sure that the Gourres were not lurking around. It had been agreed that Norette and Madame Queline would escort the fugitives to the concierge's cousin, who lived quite near.

Madame Sellier returned to her apartment as soon as the small group left the building. She prepared Fanfan's lunch and put the rest of the food on the stove to keep warm for Michel and Norette. As for herself, she was too upset to eat. Seated in her usual place, between Fanfan and Solange, she kept stirring her food mechanically, and would jump at every noise or footstep. The bell rang. It was Norette, and she was weeping.

"What's the matter?" cried Solange, rushing to her. "Did you hurt yourself?"

"No," sobbed Norette, "I . . . didn't hurt myself, but . . . Oh, Mother! Mother! They took them!"

"Yes," said Madame Queline who had come in after her, "they arrested my poor friends, just as we got to the Place de l'Odéon. My God! What a misfortune!"

Madame Sellier clutched her head in her hands with anguish.

"The poor, poor, people!" she murmured, and she couldn't hold back the tears. "What could have gone wrong? I don't understand. How did they know who they were? They didn't ask them to show their papers, did they?"

"No, they didn't," said the concierge. "They came along in a car and pulled up at the curb. Two men got out and ran after us. They took the Moscots by the arm and drew them toward the car before those poor doomed people had time to utter a syllable. . . . Monsieur Moscot managed to turn around for a second as they pushed him in, and he looked at me, looked . . . Oh, how well I knew what that look meant to say! It said 'George!'"

"But who were those men? Frenchmen? Germans?"

"Who knows? They were in civilian clothes, that's all I had time to notice. Naturally, I immediately thought of Stéphane. There was no one else who could have recognized the Moscots as we walked down the block with them. I tried to peer into the car, but they drove off at full speed, toward Boulevard Saint-Germain. . . . Damnation!" Madame Queline went on, disgustedly, "When I think that I'm keeping that rat in *my* building! What beasts they are, those Hitlerites!"

"I've had about enough of him!" Michel said, bursting into the dining room after he heard from Norette what had happened. "Mother, please let me go down and beat up that Stéphane, I want to . . ." and he made for the door; but his mother reached for him and pulled him back.

"No," she told him grimly. "This isn't the time for that sort of thing. We must first of all think of George's safety."

"George?" exclaimed Michel. "But, Mother, George is no longer in danger!"

"How do we know? I'm not sure. . . . Now that he no longer has his parents . . ."

"They'll come back, won't they?" Solange asked tearfully.

Madame Sellier pulled herself together, drying her eyes. "Yes, they'll come back, and you'll see how happy everyone will be . . . when all those whom we miss so much are with us again. . . . But now, my dear children, I must leave you for a while and go up to the Moscot apartment. The Germans seal the homes of those they arrest; they seize their belongings and send them to Germany. I must salvage for the Moscots whatever I can. . . . Won't you please help me, Madame Queline. How about their key?"

"I have it," said the concierge. "Monsieur Moscot gave it to me on the way down."

The two women left. They filled several bags with

everything of value that they could find: a silver serving set, several pieces of jewelry, a lamp, and the rest of George's clothes. Madame Sellier also took George's prize books, and Michel who had been following her around the apartment, took the printing set from the mantelpiece. They hid the things downstairs, behind the girls' beds. Then Madame Queline locked the deserted apartment, sighing mournfully. That was the end—no one could now do anything more for the Moscots.

But for Madame Sellier there remained one more difficult task. Toward six o'clock, at dusk, she asked Norette to prepare dinner, and herself went to see George at the Planquets. She found him in the shop. Armed with a huge saw, he was sawing away at a board, the workmen watching him with amusement.

"I'd like to talk to you," she said. "Where could we go?"

George led her to the room where he was going to sleep that night, and remained facing her. Falteringly she told him about the misfortune that had befallen him. "He's going to cry," she thought, her heart full of compassion. But George didn't cry. He just turned away, leaned his head against the wall, and remained motionless for a long time.

"Will they hurt them?" he finally said, not turning around.

"Oh, no! Not at all," answered Madame Sellier. "You must remember that it isn't as though they were rounded up in 1942 . . . with the others! Victory is in sight now, and there won't be time to send them to Germany—there is no question about that! They'll let them stay at the Darcy concentration camp. There," she went on, blushing with shame at telling such lies, "it isn't so bad."

"Then . . . I'll see them again?"

"You will."

George sighed with relief, and he pressed his forehead hard against the wall in an effort to master his emotions.

Madame Sellier didn't say any more, and she made no move toward him. She felt it would be wrong to touch him or try to kiss him at this moment of private grief. In a little while she got up and left, after having promised that Michel would come to see him the next morning.

But George's fate was far from settled. He couldn't stay on at the Planquet's; they expected their daughter to return any day now. More important, it was absolutely necessary that he leave the neighborhood where Stéphane prowled for more victims. Madame Sellier decided to send George away to her mother. It was there that the Moscots had chosen to go before they were taken away—that was the refuge which they had wished for their son. It was necessary, however, to avoid all risks. George didn't need an identity card, being only twelve, but he needed a different food-ration card. Madame Sellier hastened to take this up with Monsieur Lampion as soon as she returned to the house.

"I'd do it gladly," said the old man, "but, my dear woman, it isn't with that sort of thing that we are busy at the shop—we print underground newspapers! . . . Hmm . . . let me see. . . . I'll tell you what: suppose you ask Monsieur Jean."

"Why Monsieur Jean?"

"Don't you know? He no longer works at the pharmacy —not since his stay at Fresnes. He's now involved in some kind of sleight of hand—you know, false papers and such. I'm almost sure of this. . . . Why not go and see him, he's just come in."

Monsieur Jean granted Madame Sellier's request with obvious enthusiasm. "False cards? We have plenty of those!" he told her. The group he now belonged to had set up a sort of underground "city hall"—they even issued marriage licenses. "You'll have your ration card tomorrow evening," he assured her, stroking his light hair, out of habit.

And not only did he bring the food-ration card but he had attached to it a whole booklet of tickets: bread tickets, tickets for meat, for butter and other shortening. George was indeed well provided for. Mademoiselle Alice, who had a pretty handwriting, took on the task of filling out the card. Leaving George his initials, they chose for him the name of "Gabriel Moinot," born in Algeria, and residing on Rue de Liége in the ninth *arrondissement* (district) of Paris. Since the card looked too new, Mademoiselle Marie rubbed it on her kitchen floor to dirty it a bit.

Now everything was ready for George's departure. But Madame Sellier was terrified at the thought of letting George take the trip by himself. She felt that the boy was now her child, like Solange, and that she was now responsible for him. She managed to find a woman, the sister of the owner of the neighborhood dairy store, who had some business to attend to in Montluçon. She was going there within a few days, and she agreed to take George with her. Her husband being employed at the Austerlitz railroad depot, she promised to obtain a train ticket for him.

Michel went to say good-by to his friend the day of

his departure. The two took advantage of the street being deserted at that early hour and organized a "boat race" down the little curb stream, using Monsieur Planquet's loops of shavings as seacraft. Michel intentionally lost every race to George, and he also made him a present of the largest loops. When the third boat had been victoriously swallowed up by the sewer drain, George suddenly turned to Michel.

"I wasn't nice to Mother when I left," he said, his voice tight with grief. "I didn't even let her kiss me. Tell me the truth—do you think . . . do you really think that she'll ever come back?"

"Of course! . . . since my mother believes it. . . ."

"Yes," said George, "you're right, your mother did say . . ."

George took the train that same evening, accompanied by the woman. Madame Sellier couldn't sleep for a whole week. Did she do right to send him away so far? What if something happened to him on the trip—how would she know about it, now that no letters could be sent anywhere in France?

Then, a pleasant-faced old man dressed in black called on her one morning, just as she was finishing sewing a shirt. He was from Montluçon and brought news of George. The woman with whom George was traveling had tried to take advantage of changing trains at Chateauroux to barter some chicory for butter at a local grocer's. She was caught by the police: they searched her and found a dozen packages of chicory in her bag, together with several other items whose sale was forbidden. One of the policemen began to question George, and poor George, losing his head, foolishly started to cry. The policeman looked at him for a moment, frowned, then said playfully, "Say, youngster, what are you waiting for—why don't you get on that train? Can't you see it's pulling out?" George didn't wait to be told twice. He hopped onto the last coach and arrived in Montluçon without further incident.

"What a nice man!" commented Madame Sellier after recounting all this to the children during lunch. "The man had guessed the situation George was in. I'm sure of it! Our George is safe, at last! And now Grandmother can start spoiling him!"

"Will he eat chicken?" asked Fanfan wrinkling his nose.

"Chicken, and cream, and rabbit . . . to say nothing of all the fruit he'll help himself to in the orchard!"

Solange clapped her hands. Norette smiled happily. But Michel remained gloomy. He was very unhappy without his friend. The distance between home and school seemed interminable now that he walked it by himself; and when he entered the house after school, he couldn't help looking up the stairs, to the top floor, as if George were still living there. But there was no longer any George up there, nor anyone or anything else. Not even the furniture. The Germans had carted it off before sealing the apartment. The furniture belonged to the cousin of the Moscots who lived in Orange, but that was an insignificant detail to the Germans. They had paid not the slightest attention to it.

At night, when Michel thought of the empty apartment above, right over his head, his heart would tighten. Stretched out on his bed, his eyes wide open, he plotted vengeance on Stéphane. But Stéphane had been sent away two days after the arrest of the Moscots. His parents were uneasy about their son's latest action. They realized what danger their perfect little fascist, whom they themselves had shaped, represented to them now. So they shipped him off to an uncle in Touraine.

"Anyway, he won't get away with it—he'll gain nothing by his absence," Michel later said to his school chums. "The day he comes back . . ." He didn't need to finish the threat—they understood what he meant, and they remained silent and grave.

Before leaving for Allier, George had asked Michel again to become the leader in the league, and Michel had done it faithfully. He now took great pains in drawing up the leaflets. He so much wanted them to be as well written as the ones done by *Leonidas*—George. But, no matter how he juggled the eloquent phrases in his head, he somehow could never succeed in putting them down properly on paper. This caused him bitter disappointment.

Besides, he was distracted. He couldn't stop thinking about Daniel.

One day, toward the middle of May, his mother sent him to deliver an order to the dressmaking establishment for which she did work at home. On the way back to the Métro, he noticed a familiar-looking woman sitting on a bench near the entrance to the square, at the corner of Rue des Favorites. He hesitated. . . . Wasn't that the young blond woman? She looked much thinner and rather ugly, with her hair pulled back tightly and with all the buttons, but one, missing from her jacket. "Maybe I'm mistaken?" Michel wondered. But the young woman, noticing him, started slightly, and he knew then that he was right—it was she. The young woman motioned to him to come and sit down near her.

"I'm glad I saw you—I have a message for you."

Michel's heart skipped a beat. "Oh! Do they want me to help them again?"

"No, no," she said. "I mean—the message is not exactly for you. It's for the little girl who lives with you; it's from her brother."

"From Al . . . from Étienne?"

"Yes. He wants her to know that he is in a safe place and will be hiding out there."

Michel was astounded. "He's hiding? He doesn't work for the underground any more?"

"Not for the time being. We've had a bad setback. Someone put the finger on us—a member of our group whom they caught and tortured—he talked, he was scared. They uncovered our Center, and everything else. . . . Étienne escaped by the skin of his teeth, and it's a miracle that I wasn't caught. But they arrested a whole lot of us."

"What about . . . Daniel?" Michel murmured, his hero's name sticking in his throat.

The young woman looked very troubled. "Daniel was taken with the others. He was coming back from the restaurant to the café and ran smack into them. They had a photo of him. . . . Oh," she mourned, "why couldn't they have taken me in his place? I would have gladly given my life for him, and every one of us would have done the same. Now, they've got him. . . ."

"But he mustn't remain in prison," said Michel in a choked voice. "He must escape! Oh, do help him, mademoiselle, please help him!"

"We're trying to. But don't think it's so easy! If only we could . . . if only it were possible! . . ." she said, and withdrew into a sullen silence.

Michel hesitated to say anything else, and after staying a little longer, reluctantly left. He had to exert a great effort not to cry. Daniel had been arrested . . . Daniel! . . . He could suddenly see Daniel in chains, thrown into a cell from which he would never be freed, never! "I, too, would have given my life for him!" Michel said to himself, clenching his fists. But Daniel *would* get away—he was convinced of that. Daniel was stronger than all the Germans in all of Germany! Daniel couldn't be anything else but a victor!

Michel tried to think of all the stories of escape that he had read. Some prisoners tore up their sheets and made ropes, which they tied to the bars of their cell windows. "But did Daniel have sheets?" he wondered. Well, if he didn't have sheets, he'd use something else. Besides, didn't the young woman say that they were trying to help him escape?

"I'm not going to tell Mother about this," he decided. "I'll tell her only about the message from Alain, and nothing else. If I tell her about Daniel, I'll start crying, and I don't want to cry—not me! Oh, why isn't George here? If he were only here, I'd tell him all about everything, and that would make me feel a lot better. We would wait for Daniel together. . . . But, darn it, I'm not going to see George again before summer vacation —not before we go to Grandmother's in the country."

The Liberation

That year there was no normal summer vacation. On the sixth of June, half an hour after midnight, the first Allied parachutists touched ground on French soil. They took Cherbourg, they took Coustances, they took d'Avranches. Everywhere—in the east, in the west, in the south, and from Italy to Finland—the German forces were being routed. The news of victories flashed like lightning over the land, and the populace was transported with joy. Outwardly the people looked the same, but a wave of elation passed over the crowds in the streets and at the newspaper kiosks. The wildest reports passed from mouth to mouth: some maquisards encircled a whole German division; a thousand parachutists alighted in Auvergne; Hitler committed suicide. But everything seemed possible, everything seemed believable, and happy expectations rose in every heart like a fever.

The schools had been closed since the thirteenth of June. The children wandered over the city, hardly believing that there were finally no more lessons to prepare.

The rush of hope that thrilled Paris gradually took hold of the children as well. The Pirates, chased out of the Luxembourg Gardens by the Fritzes, who had set up fortifications in this park, regathered at the Seine embankment under the Carrousel bridge. Michel was now not the only one to compose leaflets. Almost all the other young patriots tried it. Bobin, Ménard, Barroux, all in the glow of new inspiration, filled page after page. And one day Mourette scored a huge success with his comrades when he read to them his proclamation, which began with the words: "Parisians! There is great news! It seems that the Russians have taken *Ôte-toi-vite* [Off-With-You-Quick]. . . ."

"It's no wonder you are the worst in the class in geography," Ménard jeered. "It's *Ossowitz,* you dope!"

"Are you sure? Our class hadn't studied that yet when school ended," Mourette said in self-defense. "We weren't up to Russia! Anyhow, all those Russian names are too complicated. Why don't the Russians call their places by simple names, like Saint-Lô or Bécon-les-Bruyères—like the rest of the world?" Mourette sighed. His friends rolled with laughter, and the fishermen sitting on the river's edge shouted at the boys not to scare the fish away with all that noise.

Madame Sellier had tacked a map of the Cotentin peninsula on the wall. It was so large that it covered nearly an entire side of the room. Each evening Solange, perched on a high stool, moved the pins she had put there the day before, showing the new advances of the Allied troops toward Paris. Michel looked at the map unbelievingly. Why, that peninsula in lower Normandie

—the one he always had such trouble tracing from his atlas—was right there on that, now crucial, map. How many times had he carefully followed the outline of its winding shores all the way from Calvados to Barfleur Point! His pencil would "dock" at Cherbourg, "sail" into the Atlantic wind, "set out to sea" directly south, and "pull in" at Avranches with dizzying speed. And there these places were on this war map—Avranches, Cherbourg—places that as school kids they had never regarded in any other way than as names printed in black against a pink background in the atlas. And these places had now become names of battles mentioned over and over again on the radio! In this bay, along that dotted line, men were risking their lives to free him, Michel. Men like Daniel, like Alain. "And what was he, Michel, doing for them?" he guiltily put the question to himself. It pained him to think that there was only one thing he could do against the enemy whom the others were fighting at the risk of their lives. And he would hurry to shut himself off in his room to compose still another leaflet, there being nothing else he could do.

Then came evenings when the radio was mute after the lights went out. For some time there had been no electricity except for five hours daily, later for only three hours, and, finally for only an hour and a half, in the evening. As soon as Madame Sellier put Fanfan to bed, she turned on the radio so as not to lose a minute of the much-awaited news report. At ten o'clock, the fateful hour, the concierge came up with old man Lampion and the Minet sisters, and they all listened to the wonderful news through the noise of air-raid warnings, which the Germans were now sounding largely for show.

Their air-raid warnings were against *imaginary* air attacks, as there were now no more approaching bombers or antiaircraft guns announcing that bombs were about to fall on some railroad station or on some remote suburb, and that people would soon be dying there.

One such evening, when Madame Queline was returning to her own place after listening to the broadcast, she found Monsieur Gourre waiting for her at the foot of the stairs.

"Well," he asked jovially, "have you been listening to the radio? What's the good news?"

She eyed him from head to foot. "Does that interest you?"

"Why not? A great deal, I assure you! The Americans are indeed powerful. . . . You don't know me well, Madame Queline—just between you and me, Madame Queline, Hitler never impressed me much."

The concierge drew herself up to her full, gaunt height and swept past him with majestic scorn. "It's too late now, my man, too late!" she said. And when Monsieur Gourre persisted, she shut the door in his face.

Two weeks later, in the middle of August, Norette went out one morning to buy a head of lettuce. Finding food to buy had become more and more difficult. Strikes had broken out everywhere, bridges had been blown up, trains derailed. Paris was cut off from the rest of the country. Things like lettuce were being sold secretly inside entrances to buildings, and one had to stand in line even for bread. Norette returned at noon, breathless with excitement.

"Oh, Mother! . . ."

"Well, where is the lettuce?"

"Mother, I heard cannon fire!"

Michel, who had been reading, threw his book in the air. "Cannon? That means they're here! They've arrived! Hurray for . . ."

"Let me finish, you! That's not all. . . . The Germans are moving out, they're leaving, they're leaving from all over! I ran into Monsieur Planquet . . . he saw them on the Place de l'Opéra, with their trucks piled high with all kinds of loot. They were marching off—an endless column of them! And Monsieur Planquet also told me that . . ."

"That's great," Madame Sellier said happily, "but where is the lettuce?"

Norette looked down at her empty hands.

"The . . . lettuce? Oh, Mommie, I don't have it any more! It must have fallen down, I mean, I must have dropped it. . . . Oh, and it was so pretty, so big!"

"It wasn't her fault!" Solange said, coming to Norette's defense.

Madame Sellier laughed. "No, it wasn't her fault; anyone could lose a head of lettuce on a day like this! . . . Come, children, let's eat!"

Michel finished his lunch (without salad) in a great hurry and went out into the street. He ran into Bobin at the crossing into Place de l'Odéon.

"Say, are you on your way there, too?" Bobin asked.

"Sure, the Pirates deserve to see all that! . . . Poor old George, if he were here . . . By the way, did you hear the cannon?"

"No, but I heard the machine guns last night. The Germans had thrown some bombs into the Trianon Hotel before they cleared out—the Trianon, you know, near our school. How those machine guns crackled, you should have heard them! And how the Fritzes must have shaken in their boots—they must have thought it was a general attack. Boy! That would have cost them plenty, if all those high-ranking slobs had still been in the Senate building! I even saw the smoke come out of the Senate windows," added Bobin with an air of importance. "We're lucky—we live right across the street from the Senate."

Michel felt definitely inferior. Why did his parents decide to live on the Rue des Quatre-Vents, a street where nothing ever happened! But he knew Daniel, and Bobin didn't! . . .

"Never mind," he boasted, himself feeling superior now, "I've seen more important things than your smoke!"

"What, for example?"

"Oh, nothing . . . They are state secrets."

"All right, keep them to yourself, but walk faster, or there won't be a single truck or fleeing German left by the time we get there."

They were about to cross Boulevard Saint-Germain when they came upon German soldiers marching in Indian file on both sides of the street. They wore new uniforms, the color of fresh green paint, and each held a rifle or a shotgun. All around them crowds of pedestrians and cyclists kept constantly on the move, while the French customers of an open-air café watched the soldiers pass with an amused and mocking expression on their faces.

"Look at that short fatso," whispered Bobin. "What a face on him! He must be telling himself . . ."

Bobin didn't finish what he was going to say. Obeying an order, the Germans goose-stepped off, and instantaneously shots were heard, mingling with the rattle of machine guns. In a flash, the café customers were on their bicycles, and the women were running wildly and pulling their children after them.

"Great!" cried Michel. "It's beginning! What a swell vacation—lots better than at Grandmother's!"

"Yes," Bobin agreed, "but this is hardly the time to get killed. If we do, we'll miss the rest of the show."

They sought safety inside a hotel entrance. About ten people were already taking shelter there and among them Michel recognized Grandfather Lampion.

"What are you kids doing here? You'd be much better off at home," he said.

"Of course not," Michel disagreed. "All the things that are going on are a real thrill for us. . . . Are they really shooting, Monsieur Lampion—with real bullets!"

"What else—you noodle-head!"

"I knew it, I knew it all the time," cried the excited Michel. "What fun! What fun!"

Old man Lampion shook his gray head. "Well, if you want fun, my boy, I guess there's going to be plenty to keep you amused these coming days."

And Michel had, indeed, plenty to "amuse" him. The next day the Germans dug in at the police headquarters, over which someone had managed to raise the French flag. The Military School, the House of Deputies, and the Senate building were all converted into German strongholds. The French Forces of the Interior, F.F.I. for short, were putting up barricades in the streets. And the people of Paris, having had their fill of suffering and humiliation at the hands of the occupation forces, joined the battle for liberation.

The Rue des Quatre-Vents—the Street of the Four Winds—had caught the fever. The tenants now no longer kept their doors shut. They wanted to be able to talk freely from floor to floor and to share the latest news instantly, true or false. The Minet ladies had emptied their bureau drawers and torn their prettiest sheets into strips for bandages. The dauntless Mademoiselle Alice had taken them to the Ambulance Service at the School of Medicine. Madame Queline invited some F.F.I. fighters to come inside and offered them large bowls of artificial coffee, holding forth all the time about the Gourres. (They no longer dared show their faces, not even to go out for bread.) Monsieur Jean and Grandfather Lampion roamed the streets from morning till night.

As for Monsieur Jean, he would have preferred to fight with the armed squads of the liberation forces, but he hadn't been trained for military service and had to content himself now with merely helping build street barricades. "The barricades," he grumbled, "that's not the same thing as fighting with arms! But, if there is no other choice . . ."

"Say, can I help you?" cried Michel, jumping up and down with anticipation.

Monsieur Jean nodded solemnly, and Michel, beside himself with joy, ran to tell his mother. Madame Sellier had hardly left the house during the past few days. She felt responsible for the little ones, and she knew that if she went out they would follow her. Michel's announcement took her by surprise and she first said a determined no. Michel exploded, "What will Alain say, what will Daniel say when they find out later that I have done nothing to help liberate Paris?" His mother looked at him with amazement. When did he acquire that sudden hard look, that manly obstinacy? How much he resembled his father, she thought with pride. And she couldn't help saying:

"All right, go liberate Paris, go ahead!"

That was just the beginning. Norette then insisted that she, too, must build barricades, and Solange followed suit, although she didn't in the least feel like venturing forth. This time Madame Sellier said a very firm no, and, to console the girls, promised to help them make a large French flag, which they would hang outside the window after the Germans left. Norette and Solange clapped their hands with glee.

Michel left with Monsieur Jean. "Where are we going?" he asked when they had met each other in the hall. "Rue de l'Ancienne Comédie," answered the young man. "They're expecting me over there—I joined the F.F.I. this morning. Here, look!" he said, unbuttoning his vest, and Michel saw a tricolor arm band pinned to the inside.

"Blue, white, red . . ." Michel said admiringly. "How beautiful! Could I get one just like that? When do I get my assignment?"

"Assignment? Thank God the F.F.I. isn't in so desperate a need that they will let the newly born help them! Be satisfied with what I'm offering you," teased Monsieur Jean.

Michel blushed up to his ears. "'Newly born' . . . 'newly born,' what nerve!" He was tempted to give Monsieur Jean a punch in the nose and leave him—him and his arm band. But what could he do by himself? So he followed Monsieur Jean, restraining his burning indignation.

The two had reached the corner when a voice called

to them from an open window, "Be careful, they're shooting!"

Monsieur Jean quickly pushed Michel behind him. Within a few seconds a volley of shots made the Place de l'Odéon impassable, bullets flying down the whole avenue.

"They aim well, those swine," said someone who could be heard but not seen. "They use any pedestrian as a target! Watch out, they're shooting from the theater! Those 'heroes' are pelting the whole square, every inch of it!"

"Thanks," Monseiur Jean called out. "Too bad," he said to Michel. "Let's turn back and take the side streets; that way we'll get there in one piece."

On the Boulevard Saint-Michel they ran into another obstacle—a tank was crouching like a huge fallen insect on the left side of the street, its gleaming gun barrels poised to shoot.

"Hell!" said Monsieur Jean. "We've got to get across somehow! Do you think we can make it?" he asked a ragged boy who was watching them from a corner house.

"You can if you make up your mind to," the boy answered indifferently. "I've crossed and, as you can see, I'm not dead yet. . . . Watch me do it. . . ."

The urchin dashed forward, crouching for safety. They heard a violently hissing sound and the boy collapsed on the edge of the sidewalk, his hands pressing against his abdomen.

"Oh, the brutes!" exclaimed Monsieur Jean. "Unfortunately, there's nothing we can do for him here," he added. "Let's make as wide a detour around that accursed tank as possible."

"But . . . what about him?" Michel pointed with horror to the bleeding boy, who was still stirring weakly.

"We'll tell the Ambulance Service on our way. . . . Let's go!"

They ran in the direction of Place Saint-Sulpice and almost at once met a group of stretcher-bearers carrying a Red Cross flag. They were walking rapidly toward the Seine. Monsieur Jean told them about the wounded boy. Then he led Michel through a maze of narrow streets. They finally reached their destination.

"What a detour," said Monsieur Jean, catching his breath. "And all this only to come back almost a full circle!" Then he pointed, saying, "Look over there, can you see the barricade?"

Michel looked. He was transfixed. . . . The huge barricade stretched across the wide street, from the bakery clear over to the vegetable store. Half of the street had been torn up; the cobblestones had been removed and piled high, reinforced with bags of sand, boards, chairs, and bedsprings. Michel even noticed a crib mattress on the bottom. But there was a wide gap to the right. Three men in shirt sleeves—one small and fair-haired, another tall and dark, and the third fat and bearded—were busy filling it. Five or six other persons, young and old, were putting up a dirt wall against the barricade. Two of them were digging up dirt from the now unpaved area and throwing shovelful after shovelful to the others, who, kneeling down, were packing the loose dirt against the barricade with their bare hands. The fat, bearded man, who seemed to be directing the operation, raised his head when he saw the new arrivals.

"Hi there!" he said to Monsieur Jean. "Listen, there

are enough of us here already. Better run over to the command post—I sent three guys over there a good quarter of an hour ago, to get us some ammunition. They should have come back by now—you'd think they were manufacturing the stuff!"

"Are you really getting some ammunition?" Monsieur Jean asked, his eyes shining with excitement.

"Only a small machine gun, five rifles, some hand grenades—that's all. And we can certainly use that machine gun! Try to hurry them up a little will you?"

Monsieur Jean disappeared into Rue de Buce. Michel remained at the barricade. No one paid any attention to him, and he didn't know what to do with himself. He looked with desperate envy at the two men with their shovels; right then he would have given everything he owned, even his printing set, to use one of the shovels. Behind him and a little farther off, a heavy-set woman with muscular arms was pulling up more cobblestones. She was loosening them with an iron pick, breathing heavily from the exertion.

A boy in shorts picked up the stones that she was prying loose and carried them to the barricade. It was Ménard. Michel rushed over, overjoyed to find him there.

"You're here, too! Great!" said Ménard. "Three cheers for us Pirates! Isn't this wonderful! Come on, get hold of some stones, quick!"

Michel, radiant, picked up a cobblestone and carried it to the short, fair-haired man, who added it to the pile. He brought him a second, a third, a sixth. The seventh time, having grown bold, he picked up three cobblestones at once, to show how strong he was.

"Why don't you form a chain," said the husky woman, wiping away the sweat trickling down her cheeks.

The two boys began to relay the cobblestones to each other.

Then the bakery door opened and a young, pretty girl in a light-colored dress appeared on the threshold. She was carrying a basket. "Would you like a drink?" she asked. "We're not going to refuse!" answered the fat, bearded man. "What awful heat!" The girl filled some glasses and passed them around.

"Ah!" remarked the tall dark man, smacking his lips. "That's a fine wine!"

"Nothing but the best," said the girl gaily. "It's a 1939 vintage—we've been saving it for Victory Day. . . . Listen . . ." she gasped suddenly, "it's started again!"

A burst of shots could be heard from the direction of Place Saint-Michel. Then there was another one—this time very close—and more followed in rapid succession. A smell of gunpowder filled the air.

"What rotten luck!" complained the fat, bearded man. "And here we are, still waiting for our ammunition! They must be fast asleep over at the command post! . . . Ah! There it comes, at last!" he cried, seeing Monsieur Jean arrive with three other young fellows. He was carrying the small machine gun and the others had the rifles and two heavy cases of ammunition, which they deposited carefully on the ground.

"That wasn't any too soon," grumbled the man with the beard.

Monsieur Jean, not listening to him, reported, "I just saw a man who had been near the Madeleine*—there's heavy fighting over there and our people are using a

* A church on the right bank of the Seine in Paris, famous for its classic architectural beauty.

cannon! The francs-tireurs have taken the city hall of the first arrondissement. . . . The Germans have the one in Batignolles, and the Americans are in Argenteuil. I heard a nurse say she saw a wounded American in a hospital over there. . . . That's it!—we've got the Fritzes on the run this time!"

Michel stared at him in utter amazement. What had become of the elegant Monsieur Jean? His rumpled hair stuck to his perspiring forehead, his pants were wrinkled, and his tie—his handsome tie—was undone and hung limply down his shirt. Monsieur Jean pulled it off altogether and threw it away with a gesture of impatience. Seeing this, Michel decided that his neighbor was indeed a changed man.

The bearded one grabbed the machine gun. "Now we're ready for them," he said, "and about time! It mustn't all end without our getting back at some of them. Let's go, men! Give it all you've got!" He loaded the machine gun, steadied it the best he could, and stuck the gun point through the aperture in the barricade, made for that purpose.

Each of the other men picked up a rifle and attached a few grenades to his belt. Then they crouched behind the barricade. Michel slipped down next to the tall dark man.

"Couldn't I have a grenade, too?" he asked timidly.

The man turned to him with a laugh. "There are hardly enough for the rest of us, *pitchounet!*—knee-high to a grasshopper and he wants to throw grenades! Stay put and try not to get in our way."

Michel threw him a glance of annihilating scorn, but he didn't have the nerve to insist. Standing on a pile of sand, he looked down the avenue with its massive trees;

the space between the trees was now empty, now crossed by darting figures of stretcher-bearers, nurses, and occasional pedestrians. The sharp discharge of pistols, the heavy barrage of rifleshots, the tac-tac-tac of the machine guns shattered the silence. Farther off could be heard the rolling boom of cannon.

Two cars passed the barricade—they were F.F.I. cars. On the top of each of them, two men lay on their stomachs, shotguns at the ready. A battle standard fluttering in the breeze was held high by a third man.

"Hurray!" roared the people on the barricade.

The man with the standard turned his head and called out something, pointing at something behind him.

"I bet he's warning us about a German vehicle," said the bearded man. "Let's keep our eyes open, everyone!"

The whole team got ready for action. The noise of a huge motor could now be heard from the right. It grew louder and louder, and a gray tank appeared, bristling with guns. The barricade machine gun was fired. The Germans fired back. A bullet whistled past Michel's head and crashed against the iron of the store shutter. Rifle bullets flew thick and heavy. Suddenly the tank gave up and disappeared between two buildings to the left, dragging itself there like a wounded beast.

"We hit it!" cried the tall dark man. "It . . ." A terrible noise drowned out his voice. The tank exploded. Thick black smoke full of flaming fragments scattered over the boulevard. What a frenzy of joy! The barricade team yelled, sang; the men punched each other happily in the chest. In his delight, the tall dark one shook Michel's hand so hard that he lost his breath from the pain.

"Look, two of them are getting away!" burst out Monsieur Jean. A couple of Germans were, in fact, running on the opposite sidewalk. They looked frantic with fear.

"The grenades!" commanded the bearded leader. A grenade was thrown. It exploded near the trees, a few yards from the fleeing figures. Another landed in the middle of the street. The Germans disappeared around the corner. The bearded man suppressed a curse.

"Damnation! We missed those two! But we got the others! What do you say, fellows? Wasn't that one hell of a strike! When the tank stops burning we'll go and help ourselves to their pistols and any other ammunition we can find. Speaking of pistols," he added, "a buddy of mine was supposed to bring me one. I wonder where he got lost. Hey, you two boys, how about finding him for me; he's probably at Marius' place, on Rue des Canettes. He's a short guy with a mustache. His name is Merlot."

"I'll go!" cried Michel.

"No, me!" cried Ménard.

"You choose between yourselves, but hurry up!"

Both boys dashed off, jostling each other.

"At last, "said Michel, "we've got something to do!"

"What about the cobblestones—wasn't that a help?" said Ménard. The Rue des Canettes was quite near. When they came to it they saw male nurses coming in their direction. They were carrying a stretcher with a woman on it. She lay there covered with a blanket, and her small feet in high-heeled slippers showed from under it. Michel didn't shudder—he had become hardened, but Ménard paled a little.

"Look, he's wounded, do you . . . do you see?"

"She's not wounded," Michel said. "She's dead—they covered her head. And it's not a man, it's a woman—she's got high heels on." And he, too, grew pale and quickly turned away.

An F.F.I. car full of bullet holes had just halted in front of the grocery store, leaving behind it a long trail of gasoline. The man who had been sitting on the hood jumped off.

"The gas is spilling out," he shouted. "The tank's been hit! We must save the gas!"

There was a flurry of footsteps, of shouts, and several women came out of the grocery carrying pots and kettles, which they quickly placed under the tank. A man stuck his disheveled head from the rear door of the car.

"We have a wounded man in here. We've got to move him out."

Two of the women left their pots and ran to the door. A little girl was sent to the first-aid station and she came back at once with a couple of nurses. They removed the patient from the car and lowered him carefully onto a stretcher. He was black and blue with bruises and there was a large bloodstain on his shirt front and one beneath his left shoulder. Michel came close to the stretcher. He looked at the wounded man and stood there paralyzed: the hurt man was Alain! Michel was so upset that, not realizing what he was doing, he grabbed Alain's bleeding hand and shook it.

"Monsieur Alain! Oh, Monsieur Alain! . . . Étienne . . ." he stammered, mixing the two names.

"Are you mad!" one of the women shouted at him fiercely, pulling him back.

"But I know him," cried Michel. "He's . . . he's my friend!"

Alain raised his head painfully. "Michel," he murmured.

"Don't worry, kid, everything is all right. It's nothing—there's nothing to make such a fuss about."

The nurses were already carrying him away. Michel hesitated. What should he do?—follow Alain or go look for the man with the revolver? Ménard decided for him. "You stay with him," he said, "and I'll go to Marius'."

Michel left with the stretcher-bearers. He hadn't quite gotten over the shock. "And what about Daniel? Where is he now?" he thought. "If Alain would only tell me . . ."

A Red Cross flag and a white streamer hung at the entrance to the first-aid station. The nurses carried Alain down a corridor and into a small room with a faint hospital smell. Bottles gleamed on metal trays on a small table. In one of the corners, a young man in a white jacket was talking quietly to an old woman preparing bandages, her glasses low on her nose. The young man in the white jacket walked over to the stretcher and, without saying anything, removed the shirt from the wounded man, felt his shoulder, his chest, here and there, asking each time:

"Does that hurt?"

Alain shook his head weakly. Then suddenly he jumped, and groaned with pain.

"Well," said the doctor, "you were lucky—if you had been hit a little lower, your number would be up. Take care of him," he said, addressing himself to a large woman who had just come into the room, "and then send him on to the Val-de-Grâce Hospital. Phone for an ambulance."

"To Val-de-Grâce?" repeated Alain, trying to raise himself. "Oh, no, not that! I want to go on fighting!"

But the doctor had already left the room. Alain fell back onto the stretcher with a sigh of pain. The nurse went to get one of the bottles, and when she returned, noticing Michel, she asked, "Who is this boy?" and said to Michel, "Leave! Out, out of here!"

"No," Alain said weakly, "let him stay awhile. . . . Stay, kid. Wait, don't go yet."

Michel withdrew to the window. With a practiced hand the woman cleansed Alain's wound and applied a temporary dressing. When that was done, Alain motioned to Michel to come closer. He obviously felt the need to talk to someone.

"Imagine!" he said to him. "What a rotten break! I had been on the barricade at Porte d'Italie. We were on our way to establish contact with the command post in the Monnaie district, when the Germans shot us down on Place Saint-Michel. Hell! That was stupid of me. It'll be my fault if things go wrong now!"

"But the doctor said you were lucky!" Michel reminded him.

"'Lucky, lucky' . . . it's obvious he didn't put himself in *my* place! Here I am, hospitalized, while the others . . ."

"And Daniel? . . ." asked Michel, no longer able to refrain from asking the question. "Was he helped to escape, yes?"

Alain shut his eyes as though in agony. When he opened them their expression was hard. "They sent him off," he said. "I don't know where . . . to Germany, I suppose. I *hope* he's alive. We've searched for him again and again, without finding a trace. I remained in hiding at the home of a comrade and then I reorganized the group."

They now heard the spluttering of a car engine outside. The nurse came running. "The ambulance is here," she announced, then added, "Have you two finished your prattle? Now, kid, off with you, quick! Tell your friend's parents that there's nothing seriously wrong with him; he's not badly hurt. Don't forget to tell them."

He took a last look at Alain and left, his heart troubled. So Daniel hadn't escaped. "They 'searched for him,'" he said to himself bitterly, repeating Alain's words. Michel was furious, "All they had to do was look harder! What had they waited for, those imbeciles? God! If only Daniel managed to get out of Germany!"

He wandered through the narrow streets, paying no attention to the whistling of the bullets. When he reached Boulevard Saint-Michel, unexpectedly, he stopped short, frozen with fear. Military trucks were burning all over the thoroughfare—they had been hit and knocked out. The store windows were riddled with bullets. Three corpses lay on the sidewalk—Germans. To the left, toward the bridge, a street battle was raging. Michel decided to try to make it home. He began to run, staying close to the buildings, darting into an entrance, running on, then seeking shelter momentarily in the next house —it was an exhausting game of hide-and-seek with the thick-flying bullets. He crossed the Boulevard Saint-Michel, barely avoiding falling under a *Tigre* tank, plunged into Rue Dupuytren and, at long last, reached his street, the Rue des Quatre-Vents, drenched in perspiration and exhausted with the long run.

He found Norette and Solange sitting at the window. They were sewing under the attentive eye of Fanfan. "We've finished the flag," cried Norette. "It's beautiful, beautiful, beautiful! We used your old shorts for blue and the red is from my bathing suit. Now we are making some Allied flags; but those are harder because of the designs."

"Where's Mother?" Michel asked.

Mother was in the kitchen, busy dying a white napkin red. Michel told her about Alain, talking very fast.

"He's alive then," she sighed with relief. "What wonderful luck!"

"He's wounded, though."

"But you told me the doctor said that it wasn't serious. . . . He did say that, didn't he? I've been dreadfully worried because we hadn't heard from him for so long. I thought he had been . . . shot. . . ."

"Oh!" said Michel, astounded.

His mother dried her red hands on her apron. "I'm going to tell Soso," she said. "Anything is better than prolonging that silence."

When Solange heard the news she put her two little hands over her heart and, holding back a sob, murmured, "I like that better."

"How come? You, too?" cried Michel.

"I'm glad," Solange said softly, "because now he won't fight any more. . . . He won't be killed!"

Michel was outraged. "That's girls for you," he said disgustedly, "cowards, miserable cowards. Not Norette, though—she wouldn't say a thing like that. But that Solange! What a wet chicken!" But his mother understood the little girl. She looked at the poor child who had been waiting daily for four years for her brother, and doubting that he would ever return. For this lonely child the war had signified one name—Alain. She kissed her tenderly and said:

"As soon as we are liberated, the two of us will go to see him, together."

"Yes," murmured Solange cuddling up to the kind woman, who had been her refuge for so long.

Big news passed from mouth to mouth that evening: the Allied columns had arrived. Some were now at Antony, at Croix-de-Berny, at Fresnes. Others were converging on the Porte de Versailles and Porte d'Orléans. Cannon fire lighted the sky over the city during the entire night. Church bells chimed the "Marseillaise." And in the morning, the cry burst like a thunderbolt from one end of the house to the other: "They are coming down the Rue Saint-Jacques! It's the French! It's Leclerc's division!"

The tenants kept rushing from one floor to another, and a current of happy madness ran through the house. There were strange scenes: Mademoiselle Alice, her hair in paper curlers, was kissing Grandfather Lampion; the concierge grabbed Monsieur Jean by the waist and the two danced a wild polka. The children scurried about as Madame Sellier, her eyes brimming with tears, hung the French flag outside her dining-room window, dreaming of her husband's homecoming.

"I'm going out," Michel called to her. "I'm going down with Monsieur Jean! Do you think George has heard the news?"

"Of course, dear. Grandmother has a radio."

"Great! Great! Good-by! I'm off!" And he loped down the stairs.

Outside, huge crowds filled the streets and the sidewalks, pouring toward the boulevard under flowing banners, moving along under the flags waving from all the balconies and even from the high dormer windows. But no noise came from that crowd, only a vibrant murmur, low and brooding, like the echo of thunder after a storm. Trembling with suspense, Michel tried to run ahead, but the people streaming from the houses swelled the throng and made the streets impassable. He had to slow down and yield to the swarming multitude.

When he finally turned the corner, the dairy store woman, who had always ignored him, now greeted him with unexpected friendliness; and a little farther, big Bobin rushed over, glad to see him. These two Pirates of the Résistance were soon joined first by Ménard and then, in turn, by Mourette, Barroux, and Roche. Yes, it was fitting that the Pirates should be together on this day —the day of France's liberation.

They lost Monsieur Jean in the crowd at the approach to the boulevard, but they didn't care. They'd get to the Rue Saint-Jacques on their own.

A file of small tanks was passing the Sorbonne University building to the welcoming shouts of the crowd. The half-tracks were filled with sun-browned men—dirty but magnificent! They looked like creatures from another world.

"*Vive la France!* Long live France!" the men roared.

An old woman threw them a bouquet of daisies. A young woman rapturously waved her small flag at them.

"We should have brought one too," said Michel. "But it doesn't really matter. Vive la France! Bravo! . . . Look, boys, there goes a big tank! Bravo!"

"Bravo! Bravo!" the Pirates kept screaming and raising their arms as high as they could.

The crowd had grown to such proportions that the vehicles couldn't proceed; they came to a complete stop. The people surrounded them immediately, holding on to the wheels, shouting, singing, weeping, shaking hands with each other.

"Hi there, kids!" called out a tall, bearded youth standing in one of the small tanks. "Hop on, there's plenty of room!"

The Pirates exchanged looks, their faces turning red. "Does he mean *us?*" stammered Ménard. "Are you sure? Should we get on?"

The young man helped them clamber onto the vehicle. It was their moment of glory! Palpitating with joy, Michel looked at the dirt-covered faces around him. The bearded youth offered him a bar of chocolate.

"Thank you, monsieur," Michel stammered.

He broke the bar of chocolate into six pieces, broke in half his own share and put one part in his pocket for his little brother. He remembered that Fanfan had not yet experienced the marvelous taste of chocolate.

"Excuse us, gentlemen, for not saying anything at the moment," Ménard said politely, his mouth crammed with the treat, "but it's so good, we don't want anything to take our minds off the taste!"

The youth laughed uproariously and the other men followed suit. Ménard blushed violently. "What was so funny about what he had said?" he wondered.

"We, too, accomplished a few things!" he blurted out provocatively. "We are the 'Pirates of the Résistance' and we issued leaflets, all of last year!"

"Did you say 'Pirates'?" the youth exclaimed, slapping

his leg with mirth. "That's pretty good, and if that's how it is, I say three cheers for the Pirates, my friend!"

And there was more laughter, while Ménard, his face crimson red, choked on his chocolate.

At that instant there was a burst of shots, their racket rising above the ecstatic "Vives."

"There are snipers on the Sorbonne roofs!" someone cried. "It must be the *miliciens.** The filthy traitors!"

"Ah, the filthy traitors!" the crowd echoed, looking up at the roofs.

"For God's sake, get down, lie low," another voice shouted.

The crowd lurched. Several persons threw themselves flat on the pavement. A child began to cry. But the men in the half-tracks remained calm and continued their merriment. The Pirates followed suit—after all, they too were soldiers, in a way.

The tanks were moving again. The fusillade had subsided. The vehicles were rolling toward the Seine, followed by the multitude shouting its bravos, singing, yelling. Michel managed to squeeze himself into a small space near the driver.

"Say, kid, do you think you could phone someone for me?" the driver asked him, flinging away his half-smoked cigarette.

"Yes, of course."

"Well, would you phone my wife for me? The number

* Frenchmen who had volunteered to serve as militia with the German occupation forces; they were justifiably regarded by their countrymen as the most despicable of all collaborators with the enemy.

is *Marcadet* 16-53—Madame Dupin. Can you remember that?"

"Marcadet 16-53, Madame Dupin," Michel repeated conscientiously, recalling the distant day when he repeated, in the same manner, the names of the streets that led to the *Rendez-Vous* café.

"Ask to speak to my wife," the soldier said. "Tell her that we are continuing to advance, that we were only passing through Paris. Tell her that you saw me and that I looked well, that I'll soon get leave."

"I'll tell her all that—you can rely on me," said Michel fervently, and turning to his comrades, he called out, "Hey, fellows, did you hear that? I'm going to phone Madame Dupin, Marcadet 16 . . . 16 . . ."

" . . . 53. Don't you go and forget the number!"

"You are a smart one, Boucot!" cried the youth now sitting on the floor of the half-track. "How about it, Pirates? If you happen to live in this neighborhood, could you visit my home and give my mother a message?"

"I'll go! Me! Me! Me!" shrieked the Pirates, raising their hands frantically, as though they were in the classroom.

"All six of you may go, if you want to; the more the merrier. It's Rue des Quatre-Vents, number 24—Madame Quel . . . what's the matter?" he asked, seeing Michel gesticulate frantically.

Michel swallowed hard. "But, but, that means you are . . . does that mean you are her son? That's where we live, 24 Rue des Quatre-Vents! That's our house!"

He devoured the young man with his eyes, and, searching his memory, recalled a lanky, restless youth who used to look down on him, Michel, because he was already sixteen and worked in a garage. How could he have recognized that raw youth in this conquering hero in uniform? The youth looked at him intently for a long moment, an expression of amusement on his face.

"Now I remember!" he finally said. "You must be the Sellier kid—the family on the third floor. How you've shot up in these four years!"

He shook Michel's hand the way men shake hands. The other Pirates looked on with awe. Michel was bursting with pride.

"I'll go there right away!"

"Us too!" cried the others.

And the whole bunch tumbled out of the vehicle with equal eagerness.

"You aren't going to make both calls," Bobin warned Michel angrily, when they had at last crossed over to the other side of the street, pushing their way through the unyielding mass of people. "If you call on Madame Queline, I'll telephone the other lady."

"But it's me they both asked," Michel protested.

"Maybe, but that's not fair. . . . Let's go, fellows; we're going to phone Madame Dupin without him."

Ménard, Mourette, Roche, Barroux followed Bobin to a café. But all the cafés were closed.

"Maybe if we knock they'll open up?" suggested Bobin.

"They should, since it means doing a soldier a favor, and one from Leclerc's division at that!"

"All the café owners must have gone out," said Ménard. "Why can't we phone from my house—I'll call the number."

"All right . . ." sighed the others, resigned but deeply disappointed.

Michel had left them to hurry to the Rue des Quatre-Vents. He elbowed people aside paying no attention to their protestations. At the intersection of Place de l'Odéon he heard wild shouting. In an army truck absurdly knocked out of shape, sat five Germans squeezed together, five Germans without their uniform belts, without epaulets, and heaped together like so many misshapen objects. The crowd kept up the shouting. Michel moved on but kept looking back and gaping at the Fritzes. He wanted to join in the yelling but felt as though someone was prodding him on. He repressed the yell that he was about to emit, turned around, and proceeded slowly across the square.

He stopped short in front of his house, amazed. Was that the right house—*his* house? The front of the building was covered with numerous flags: French, English, American, Russian, and tricolor flags studded with white stars, the colors on some of them looked fresh and childish. All the windows were decorated with flags except those of the Moscot apartment and the Gourre windows, whose shutters remained tightly closed. Michel recognized, flowing from the third-floor balcony, the blue cloth of his old shorts. Last but not least, on the ground-floor level near the concierge's quarters, was displayed a white placard with the following words printed in red and blue letters:

LONG LIVE THE LIBERATION!

LONG LIVE FRANCE!

WE IN THIS HOUSE *RESISTED!*

Dressed in her best, Madame Queline was busy contemplating her handiwork. Michel threw his arms around her neck.

"Good news!" he cried. "Guess what it is!"

"Would you please not wrinkle my dress!" she grumbled, freeing herself. "What now—what other good news is there? Haven't we already heard enough for one day? Except for the return of my son, I can't imagine what else remains!"

"Well," said Michel, "that's it!"

Red spots appeared on the concierge's long face. She swayed as if she were going to fall and steadied herself against the placard. The placard came down with a sharp little noise.

"My . . . little son," she murmured, "my little one, my little boy! Tell me, did you see him? Where is he?" she exclaimed, grabbing Michel's arm. "Go on, talk you little dunce!" She kept shaking him with all her strength, and Michel, tossed back and forth, told her as best he could about his encounter with the young Queline.

"Tell me, did he look handsome?" she asked. "Did he look well? Did he seem happy? . . . Darn it, why didn't I go down to Rue Saint-Jacques instead of staying here to put up this silly placard? Now it's torn—what a waste!

Come, boy, repeat everything once more, everything you have just told me—start from the beginning!"

When Michel had finished repeating for the third time his short story, the concierge said, tidying her bun, "I'm going to inform the tenants." Her voice shook.

But not very many of the tenants were home just then. Norette and Solange had gone out in the company of Grandfather Lampion, and there was no one at the Selliers except the two Minet women and Madame Sellier, who had just returned from town with Fanfan. But it was enough for Madame Queline to share her joy with those three sympathetic souls. Madame Sellier was thrilled, the old ladies asked question after question, and Michel had to tell his story for the fourth time.

"He's become handsome, very handsome!" the concierge kept repeating. "Ah, that doesn't surprise me! If you had only seen his pictures when he was little! I'll show them to you, but not right now. My! I hardly know what I'm doing! What a day of triumphs! If only my husband were alive!"

Madame Queline wept and laughed, and the three women wept and laughed with her.

"I've been meaning to ask you," said Mademoiselle Alice when everyone had calmed down, "what do you suppose the Gourres are up to—I passed their place not long ago and there wasn't a sound. It seems odd that . . ."

"Do you think they might have . . . committed suicide?" wondered Madame Queline.

"What are you saying? How could all three of them have committed suicide?" Madame Sellier said. "That's impossible."

"Why? On the contrary, the more I think of it, the more

likely it seems. They've been shaking with fear these last few days. Let's knock on their door and see."

"Let's wait till tomorrow," urged Madame Sellier. "Maybe they'll decide to come out in the meantime."

But the Gourres did not come out the next day, and none of them responded to the concierge's repeated and loud ringing of their bell. Everyone followed hesitantly behind her when she let herself into their apartment. They found the place deserted. The closets were empty and the drawers open. Everything showed signs of a hasty departure. The remainder of a large ham had been forgotten on the table.

"They've fled!" cried the concierge. "And just look at that ham! Those traitors certainly didn't stint themselves! But how did they manage to leave without my knowing it? I've hardly left my place. Let me see . . . ah, wait—someone rang me last night and asked me to pull the cord for the outside door. I thought it was Monsieur Jean."

"Monsieur Jean spent the night on the barricades," said Mademoiselle Alice. "He came in only this morning—you saw him."

"How stupid of me!" lamented the concierge. "No, on second thought, it was your fault, Madame Sellier—if you hadn't advised me to wait till today, I would have gone up there yesterday evening. Just think, to have let them get away without even telling them to their mean faces what we thought of them! Why, I'd be willing to join the fighting to make up for my blunder!"

She was smoldering with rage. To calm her, Madame Sellier began to talk about her son. "He must have looked very handsome indeed," she said sweetly, "standing there in that tank and being acclaimed by all of Paris! And, think of it—he'll soon come to see you! Think of your fine son, Madame Queline, forget the Gourres! I assure you that no matter where they are now, they are shaking from head to foot with fear. We'll probably never see them again, and it's just as well. Now, if you'd be kind enough to show us those baby pictures of your fine son . . ."

They all went down to the concierge's quarters, and while the old ladies were going into ecstasy over the photograph of a fat infant seated on a fat pillow, Michel reached in his pocket for the piece of chocolate he had saved for Fanfan. He went up to the third floor, four steps at a time, and hurried inside to his little brother.

"Look what I have, my Fanfan," he said. "This is for you! It is real chocolate, éclair chocolate, the kind I told you about in my story."

"But there's no dripping cream," Fanfan observed, staring at the chocolate suspiciously.

"There'll be cream later," cried Michel. "Eat it, Fanfan, you'll see how delicious it is . . . because now it's all over—understand? You are free, I am free, George is free, we are all free, at last!"

And Michel looked gravely at the large flag waving from the window in the sunlight.

Conclusion

The camp in which Monsieur Sellier had been a prisoner was one of the first to be liberated. He had landed at Le Bourget Airport, and his wife and children came to meet him at the Hotel Lutétia. When Madame Sellier saw his emaciated face in the crowd, she had to let him come toward her, for she was so stricken that she couldn't move. Michel and Norette threw themselves in his arms, overcome with happiness and tears, but Fanfan pouted and hid behind his mother, whimpering:

"I don't want that man to kiss me."

Just the same, it was a wonderful reunion. When Madame Sellier was falling off to sleep that night, she didn't feel weighed down by the heavy burdens that she had carried alone for the past four long years. In the future, no matter what happened, there would be the two of them to face it.

Monsieur and Madame Moscot never came back. No one knew what had become of them, despite the efforts Monsieur Sellier later made, through the Red Cross, to find them. George was alone in the world. He had had no other relatives than his Uncle Eugene. But this uncle had died in a concentration camp. The Selliers decided to have George live with them and to raise him as their own son. Solange was no longer staying with them. After her brother recovered from his injury, she went back to live with him in the apartment next door. But she had become so used to sharing her days with Norette that, whenever possible, she came to knock at her door. And when Madame Sellier happened to forget to kiss the little girl in greeting, her face would cloud over as in the past.

Daniel never returned. They found his grave in a shallow cave near Amiens, where the Germans had executed him. He had been a college professor, and the following April his memory was honored at an impressive ceremony at the Sorbonne. All the tenants of the house on the Rue des Quatre-Vents attended, from little Fanfan to Grandfather Lampion. The old man looked splendid in the black, holiday suit he wore for the occasion. Seated next to his mother, Michel listened to all the speeches without missing a word. The speakers praised Daniel the teacher, Daniel the scholar, Daniel the hero of the Résistance, but the Daniel whom Michel remembered was the man with the determined look who had said to him at the *Rendez-Vous,* on a certain fateful day, "Well done!" Michel solemnly vowed to himself to remain forever loyal to this man.

A few days later he visited Monsieur Planquet's carpenter shop. His father was there smoothing a board with that marvelous plane, and, as before, the shavings were flying in all directions. Michel gathered a few and went outside to float them down the curb streamlet. He didn't take the trouble to steer them.

"That's strange," he said to himself, "but this is no longer fun. Maybe it's because I'm too old now. . . ."

He threw the rest of the shavings into the gutter and went home in a pensive mood.